I don't know how long I lay there, relapsing into mindless drea

Suddenly, the _____ raw grating sound. _____ was a fleeting sha_____ of a bird. But some _____ animal instinct moved me. I flung myself backward—under the overhanging balcony. Where I'd been lying only a second before, a huge pot crashed down, flying to pieces in great jagged shards as it hit the terrace.

A chunk of stone, razor-sharp, had knifed into my shin.

Henley burst out of the house, Maria with him, her dusky face full of terror. Thrusting them aside to leap the steps came someone I had never seen before, yet I knew him instantly. It could only be Michael Cromwell.

Time seemed to catch and hold, like a white thread on black wool, while Michael and I stared at each other. . . .

THE SECRETS OF CROMWELL CROSSING was originally published by Lancer Books, Inc.

The Secrets of
Cromwell Crossing

DAOMA WINSTON

PUBLISHED BY POCKET BOOKS NEW YORK

FOR MURRAY

THE SECRETS OF CROMWELL CROSSING

Lancer Books edition published 1965

POCKET BOOK edition published September, 1976

This POCKET BOOK edition includes every word contained in
the original edition. It is printed from brand-new plates made
from completely reset, clear, easy-to-read type.

POCKET BOOK editions are published by
POCKET BOOKS
a division of Simon & Schuster, Inc.
a GULF+WESTERN COMPANY
630 Fifth Avenue
New York, N.Y. 10020.
Trademarks registered in the United States
and other countries

ISBN: 0-671-80693-9.

Printed in the U.S.A.

Chapter *ONE*

"THAT'S OUR fence," Jamie said. "The beginning of our land. If you look to the right, high up on the mountain, you'll get a glimpse of the house as we go around the next curve."

But, hearing the nervousness in his voice, knowing that he had become more and more tense as we drove across the desert to our destination, I looked at Jamie instead.

"Not at me, Robin," he barked. He slammed on the brakes so suddenly that I was flung forward and had to catch myself against the dashboard.

All his winning boyishness, the boyishness that had made it possible for me to trust him, seemed to have fallen away. I sat back, ruefully moving my bruised wrist, wondering, and not for the first time since we had begun the trip from Los Angeles, if I had done the right thing.

"There," Jamie said urgently. "There it is, Robin."

I followed the motion of his hand, and my breath caught in my throat. Beyond the wicked prongs of the barbed-wire fence lay miles and miles of wind-eroded plains, buttes, canyons, and startling outcroppings of sculptured rock, that ended in the swift rise of rugged mountains.

Among the hills, the house seemed to sit at the edge of the world. Though it was still so far away, so high, I could see it clearly through the thin dry air. The huge building of gray stone sprawled on a natural shelf which

5

cut into a sheer cliff. Wavering tips of cedar and spruce surrounded it. High above the dark roof, a brilliant sunset painted the bald mountain peak a harsh unnatural red, but the house itself, by some trick of light, was wrapped in shadow, except for dozens of blank staring windows that pitched fragments of sunlight back at us, fragments like flashing demon eyes.

That was my first glimpse of the mansion named Cromwell Crossing. It was big, shadowed, and, already, somehow frightening.

I wondered again if I'd been right in listening to Jamie's persuasions. His wide-apart blue eyes had been so honest, his voice so sincere. I had been reassured by the boyish triumph of his smile when he cried, "You won't be sorry, Robin."

But, as we neared Cromwell Crossing, Jamie had changed. It was as if some seed already within him had begun to develop, to thicken and flower with every mile that passed. A taut, hard, nervous impatience drove him so that the smiling young Jamie I had known for just a little more than three weeks seemed to be disappearing before my eyes.

As I had before, I repressed my sudden sense of uneasiness, reminding myself that I knew exactly what I was doing. Though he had tried to at first, Jamie had not been able to draw me into this venture completely blindfolded. If I had few facts, at least I had no illusions either. We had our definite understanding, and he had already proved many times that he would live up to it.

All I needed now was a little courage, and I would finally have what I had wanted, what I had promised myself, all my life. The trouble was that I knew, if no one else did, that I did not possess a great deal of courage. From my earliest days, I had learned to walk warily. Yet, I had learned, too, from hard necessity, to act out a convincing image of the inner strength I had never felt.

My pixie-cut hair, once a brutal red, had deepened to burnished copper, but reckless people might still make the mistake of calling me "Red." My eyes were slightly slanted over high cheekbones; they were an odd green that sometimes shaded to black. A green-eyed redhead is a stereotype which signifies not only temper, but also defiance and bravery in even the most timid girls. So, although I was small—a shade over five feet tall and slender as a model of petite dresses had to be—the imputation of my coloring was a great protection to me. I knew I would have to draw on that protection now.

As Jamie drove on, I said, "The house is so big. I never dreamed it would be so imposing."

Jamie laughed, obviously pleased that I was impressed. "But I told you, Robin. Didn't you believe me when I explained about the money? There's plenty of it, and always has been. The Cromwells have the magic touch. It's there, and I want it, and I'm not going to wait forever."

Once more, I sensed the hungry impatience in him— I understood it because I had often experienced it myself. Jamie wanted to be free. To be free meant to be independent. To be independent meant having. . . . But I stopped myself from carrying that thought further. The implications frightened me. My independence was the reason I was here with Jamie who was almost a stranger. All at once, I wasn't sure my motive was good enough.

Jamie, peculiarly attuned to me as he sometimes was, asked, "You're not scared, are you? You know you can do it." And added slowly, "Besides, you can't change your mind now."

I gave a little laugh. "Of course, I can do it. Don't worry about that. But you didn't say you'd grown up in a mountainside castle."

"And that's just what the people in town, in Cromwell

Crossing, call it. They're kidding, of course. But it's what they say." He grinned, his face suddenly relaxed, boyish again.

"Did your father build it?"

"My grandfather." Again, Jamie grinned. "Quite a bunch, the ancestors. Get my father to tell you about them sometimes. He's a sucker for family talk, old Sebastian is."

"And what about the family now, Jamie? Who'll be there?"

"You'll see them soon enough," Jamie said, and the mask of nervousness slid over his face again, narrowing his pale-blue eyes, tightening his mouth.

He had given me the same answer before. He seemed to refuse to understand that the more I knew, the better I would be able to do what he expected of me. Still, I didn't pursue it. As Jamie said, I would know soon enough.

Jamie went on, "That business—Sebastian's being all wound up in family stuff—it makes me sick. But it's going to help. It's going to work for us. Old Sebastian wants him a grandson, and he wants one fast. This generation isn't enough for him. He's got to see the next, too. I guess that's why——" Jamie's voice trailed off.

I prompted him. "That's why *what?*"

But he just shook his head, his mouth grim.

I clasped my hands in my lap and let the cool air, so blessedly different from the recent hot desert wind, brush my cheeks.

Our brief glimpse of the house was long behind us. The car sped on through a deepening lavender twilight which lay like a faded coverlet on clumps of mesquite and sage and hung in a misty shroud on the proximate mountains.

The tires abruptly changed from their monotonous

thrum to sing higher and shriller. We were crossing a long narrow bridge. Below us, a thin gleam of turgid brown water cut a meandering course through the almost dry river bed that spread wide between broken curved banks.

"And that is our Cromwell River," Jamie explained, "where the ancestors first set up shop here. They had the ferry. They only gave it up when the first bridge was built."

"And when was that? It doesn't look now as if you'd ever needed a ferry here," I told him.

"I guess they built it approximately fifty years ago. Sebastian says it was an old wooden thing that got flooded out every couple of years. The river's generally just about dry in August. But, in the spring, it fills up with runoff from mountain snows."

"And the town, Jamie?"

"Oh, yes, Cromwell Crossing—our immortality," he replied dryly. "What there is of it, and there isn't much, is just ahead."

I sat up straighter, braced against the smooth upholstery, forgetting the luxurious comfort of the huge convertible that Jamie seemed to take so much for granted. I knew we must be almost to the house.

The twilight had gone, like a lamp suddenly switched off, leaving an empty silent dark. Not far away now, crouched like huge sleeping animals, the mountains waited, sheltering the big old mansion which had flashed a dozen gleaming demon eyes into the sunset.

We hurtled past a few shadowy shapes I couldn't identify. A block of neon signs sprang up. I read "Drugstore," "Café," "Gas," before they disappeared.

"And that was Cromwell Crossing," Jamie said.

"I wish we could stop for a minute. I'd like to look around," I told him, knowing he would ignore any request from me.

Jamie hadn't paused, even for a short rest, since early afternoon in Santa Fé. There, he'd surprised me by lingering, almost as if he didn't want to go on. While I wandered under the dusty cottonwood trees, viewed the Rio Grande, window-shopped in the narrow crooked streets, and looked at the square adobe houses with their tiled red roofs gleaming under the sharp blue of the sky, I wondered if he were thinking of changing his mind. I knew I wouldn't try to dissuade him. If he wanted to return to Los Angeles, I would go, and gladly. I would have had a pleasant trip to Santa Fé, and I promised myself that one day I'd return to walk the winding streets again.

But, finally, Jamie told me that we had better go on. I realized that he had sensed my restlessness, my resentment of our passage which was so swift that I was barely able to see the strange and beautiful country. Therefore, the stop in Santa Fé.

I humored him now as he had humored me then. I said, "Of course, you're anxious to get home."

"No," Jamie told me bitterly. "I'm never anxious to get home. But there's no use stalling. I want to get the whole thing over with as soon as I can."

"It's hard to understand people," I said thoughtfully. "You have a family and a place to belong to, and you sound as if you hate it, Jamie. And I guess those are the two things that I always wanted more than anything else."

"I was there. That doesn't mean I belonged," Jamie answered shortly. Before I could comment, he went on, "The lights on the left mark our landing field."

"You mean your family has a plane?"

Jamie nodded. "Old Sebastian used to do a lot of flying. Cromwell Enterprises, his business interests, kept him hopping."

"What are the enterprises?"

"Oil, gas leases, ranches." Jamie shook his head vaguely. "I don't even know what all. I never cared." He seemed to change the subject deliberately. "The house is only five winding miles or so from town, so you'll have plenty of chances to explore. Besides, Uncle Ned lives there. We'll go visit him tomorrow most likely."

I laughed. "Now you've told me one thing about your family. At least, I know you have an Uncle Ned."

Jamie's teeth flashed in a grin. "And you know it wrong, too. Uncle Ned is a kind of stand-in uncle. He's old Sebastian's closest friend, and his doctor. Aunt Belinda is his wife. They have the Cromwell house in town. But Sebastian will tell you all about that. Just give him the chance."

"I will, Jamie. You can be sure."

"As a matter of fact, Aunt Belinda is the first one to convince. She's a real type, a walking example of all the old-fashioned virtues, Robin."

A quick pinch of fright kept me from asking any more questions. Perhaps, after all, Jamie was right. It was better not to be too well prepared.

"It was Aunt Belinda who did the mothering," Jamie said absently.

I waited, but Jamie didn't go on.

At last I said, "You must be very fond of her."

He only shook his head.

The road lifted, swooped, curved away before us. I realized sharply that we hadn't passed any other cars, hadn't seen any houses, any lights, any living thing since Cromwell Crossing. I braced myself against another pinch of fright.

"It's so quiet, Jamie, so empty," I heard myself saying breathlessly.

"It's the end of nowhere," he agreed. "See why I have to do this?"

"I can see why you'd want to live in San Francisco maybe, but——"

Jamie interrupted me. "Here we go, Robin. This is it."

We made a swinging right turn off the highway.

I caught a brief glimpse of two huge gray stone pillars that braced the gravel road like soldiers at attention. Then I was flung back as the car began to climb, spinning showers of pebbles behind us.

The stars seemed closer, a scattering of diamonds on a swatch of blue velvet that stretched across the tips of tall black trees.

I gasped as we slewed around a hairpin turn. Then suddenly the steep grade fell away, and the shadowy spruces were gone.

Jamie braked the car to a slow stop in a clearing.

"Cromwell Crossing," he said. "This is it."

"I'm glad that ride is over," I told him, unclenching my fists. "That road is a bad dream."

"It's been fixed up a lot," Jamie said. "You should have seen it before."

"I'm glad I didn't." I took out a comb and quickly fluffed my wind-tousled hair. I touched lipstick to my suddenly dry mouth.

"You're not scared, are you?" Jamie asked softly.

"Should I be?" I demanded.

"No. But remember—more than on anything else, it depends on you."

"It'll be all right, Jamie," I said, pretending much more assurance than I felt.

"Then let's go."

I touched the gold ring on my finger. That, at least, was real, I thought, as I followed him from the car toward the silent waiting house.

I had a quick confused impression of size and shadow, of sprawling wings and balconies and tall windows edged with ribbons of subdued yellow light. I remembered my first glimpse of the manor at Cromwell Crossing, the blank staring windows that had flashed bits of sunset at me across miles and miles of red plains, reflections like a dozen demon eyes full of wild warning.

The big dark house that was Jamie's home, and that he hated, seemed to exude a strange air of melancholy. I felt it move out to claim me with thick dark waves. I stopped in mid-step, as though those waves were actually holding me.

"What's wrong?" Jamie asked.

I took a long slow breath, forcing back the words I wanted to cry out; not allowing myself to say: "Let's go, Jamie. Let's just go away from here." Instead, I answered, "Just caught my heel," and went on.

I promised myself that I wouldn't let my silly imagination spoil everything.

We had reached the foot of the broad stone stairs when the heavy door was flung back, revealing a slim silhouette against a dim background, and a young voice shouted: "Jamie! Jamie, darling, is that you? We've been waiting for hours and hours. Honestly, I never knew such a long day. Just wait till I get the switch, and——"

As two brilliant beams flashed on from over the wide door, the quick words faded away. A moment of frozen silence seemed to stretch into eternities of time.

Jamie and I were caught in the shafts of blinding light. Automatically, I reached for his hand, and as I felt his fingers close around mine, I thought how right that was, how good. Yet, at the same time, I was paralyzed, impaled, stunned, like an actress who had forgotten her lines and waited, lost and helpless, for prompting, while she sensed from beyond the footlights the rage of an unseen audience.

Then the quick words came again, a joyful scream that melted the frozen silence. "Oh, Jamie, I'm so glad you're home. These months have been just awful." The

silhouette, changing as it plunged into the light, became
a tall laughing girl.

Jamie let go of my hand and raced up the steps to
meet her halfway. He hugged her to him, laughing,
"Annetta, you've grown two inches! You're one gorgeous
babe."

There was more of it and, while I waited, my fingers
cold around my purse, I knew this was the beginning. I
had come that far, to Cromwell Crossing, and committed
myself, and I couldn't change my mind and turn back.
Beyond Jamie and the girl on the steps, the house seemed
to swell and darken against the star-sprinkled sky.

Then Jamie held out his hand, calling in a soft drawl
that was new to me, "Robin, come on, here's my sister."

I went slowly to join them, the precise kind of diffi-
dent smile on my mouth. I didn't have to pretend.

Jamie's arm went around my shoulders. His voice was
full of a sweet, shy boyishness as he said, "Annetta, this
is Robin. This is my wife."

Chapter *TWO*

ANNETTA WAS still, staring at Jamie. Then she turned
to me. I caught a brief unbelievable glint of malice from
black eyes that became as expressionless as jet over a
petulant child's mouth.

Then Annetta spun away, crying, "Come in, come in.
Wait until Sebastian hears. And why didn't you tell us,
Jamie?" At the door, but not looking back, "Robin? So

that's your name. Robin." She repeated it slowly, as if tasting it and not liking its flavor. Then, "I hate all names beginning with 'R.' Rita, Ruth, Rose—all of them."

I heard Jamie's indrawn breath hiss, but Annetta rattled on, "And Robin, too. So I'll call you Bobby. Okay, Bobby?" She turned, smiling brilliantly.

I didn't have to answer Jamie's sister because she darted ahead, shouting, "Sebastian, come on. Meet Jamie's wife."

Jamie had closed the door behind us. He gave me a rueful grin. "She's a wild one, as you can see. But you can't blame her, growing up alone in this house." He smoothed his sandy curls and straightened his jacket and took my hand. "Now, let's go tell Sebastian the good news."

But I hung back, looking around the big entrance hall. The floor was carpeted with a thick dark rug. A wide flight of steps spiraled against the wall at my right. At my left, there obviously was the reversed side of another flight of steps, and, in the slanted alcove beneath them, were huge wooden planters holding small exotic trees.

Jamie must have followed my puzzled glance. He said, "All that stuff was moved out of the conservatory when it was rebuilt last year into Sebastian's wing."

"But the steps, Jamie?"

"They're an old story. My grandfather had the house put up with the front facing the valley. Later, Sebastian decided that, since the cars have to park out back, we should have a front entrance here, too. I guess we have the only place in the state with two front doors. It's typical of the Cromwells."

I looked up for a quick glimpse of mahogany balconies spiraling upward in rose-colored light before Jamie led me impatiently into the main hall, where, yes, again, I saw a broad stairwell and polished wooden banisters.

I hardly had time to notice the huge dark paintings

in wide golden frames that lined the walls, and the rows and rows of potted plants in round wooden planters that filled the corners.

Annetta was shouting, "Here they are, Sebastian!"

The double doors to the north wing flew back. Sebastian Cromwell, Jamie's father, stood in the doorway looking at me. As soon as I saw him, my heart sank. I realized that I was seeing a strong man who had withered and wasted from illness.

Sebastian Cromwell was tall, well over six feet, and broad-shouldered. But his big body had thinned down to gauntness. The gauntness was stressed by the loose dark jacket he wore over a white-on-white shirt, and by the black bow of the gambler's tie at his wrinkled throat. Straight-cut frontiersman's pearl-gray trousers flapped at his long legs as he moved very slowly toward us. His dark-blue eyes were piercing and full of surprising youth as they surveyed me in a look that was not at all fatherly. But those young-man's eyes were set deep in dark pockets, underscored with faded mauve patches. His hair was a mixed gray and white. His mouth, its slow smile barely tipping the corners—the smile that I was soon to know very well—was faintly bluish.

Sebastian said, "Here you are then, Jamie, and it's good to see you after all these months." Every word came slowly, preceded and followed by a pause, the speech of a man who had to conserve his breath.

I turned a puzzled look on Jamie. I couldn't understand why we were here now that I'd seen Sebastian Cromwell.

Jamie's father went on, "And here's your bride, Jamie. Come on, girl. Let these old eyes have a look at you."

I smiled to myself. As if he hadn't already looked, and looked hard, too, in those first few seconds.

But Jamie went ahead, laughing, to hug Sebastian

gently; then, gathering me in, he rocked us both in brief bonds of warmth.

Behind Sebastian, I saw Annetta watching, her face expressionless.

"This is my Robin," Jamie said.

"Her name is Robin, Sebastian, but I've already told her I'm going to call her 'Bobby,' " Annetta cried.

A quick shadow seemed to touch Sebastian's face. Brief as it was, it again brought back to me the waiting melancholy of the big old house, a melancholy that even soft light and thick carpets couldn't hide.

But then Sebastian smiled at me. Once more, his dark-blue eyes peered from purple patches to sweep me from top to toe. I could see no sign of disapproval, yet I sensed his reservations.

First impressions, my quick emotional response to people, had always been important to me. I had hoped Sebastian would accept me on sight, accept me just because I was Jamie's choice. I was disappointed now, though I hadn't really expected it to be so easy. But I couldn't blame him. He was, after all, a wealthy man. He had to be sure that his son had married safely and well.

It was my job to convince him. That was why Jamie had brought me to Cromwell Crossing.

Sebastian was saying, "Well, Jamie, at least you've proved that you have inherited the Cromwell taste for good-looking girls."

"Haven't I?" Jamie asked, laughing.

I hoped that I was able to keep my bewilderment well hidden. Jamie, with his bitter little hints, hadn't prepared me for so warm a welcome. Nor was I prepared for the change in Jamie himself. He was no longer a sullen twenty-four-year-old fighting a domineering father. He had become the prodigal son, come home to show off his new wife.

"Pretty as a picture," Sebastian went on in his slow way. "But a little minute of a girl." His eyes seemed to measure me. "I hope you're sound, Robin."

"Small packages contain lots of good solid things," I told him pertly.

He laughed. "Often true."

"You're standing too long, Sebastian," Annetta cut in.

He nodded, not looking at her. "Yes, and we mustn't stay here. What am I thinking of? Maria's in the kitchen trying to salvage a small celebration supper she prepared hours ago, Jamie. You had best take Robin in to introduce her. Then you'll want to wash up after the long trip. And, since it's more than your homecoming, tell Henley, he's most likely out there too, to chill two bottles of champagne."

Beyond his shoulder, I saw Annetta roll her dark eyes up in a mock faint and draw her mouth into a horrible grimace while the facets of beautiful earrings (which must be diamonds, I thought) flashed rainbows at me.

Annetta caught me watching her, and the grimace faded into a brilliant smile. She was about eighteen, I thought, seeing her at last in a clear light, with the distortion of shadows gone. Her eyes were the bottomless dark of black currants. Her skin was the kind of soft creamy white that neither burns nor tans. She was beautifully tall, an advantage which, being short myself, I appreciated more than most. She had straight shoulders, flat narrow waist, long slim legs. Her clothes, a long-sleeved black jersey and skintight black stretch pants, emphasized her slenderness. But I sensed a robust quality about her, the suppleness of a girl who had grown up with brothers, and had been a tomboy much longer than most hoydens. Still, there was a sweet touching awkwardness in her manner and movements, an adolescence, which made me certain that only a trick of lighting had caused me to read malice in her first glance toward me.

It could only have been a trick of shadow, I told myself again as Annetta, pulling at Sebastian's arm, said, "Come on, you've really been on your feet too long. You go and rest. I'll lead the parade to the kitchen."

Her father allowed himself to be drawn aside, nodding at us. "I'll be in the study."

Annetta pranced ahead of us, swinging her hips drum-major style. "Here comes the bride!" she shouted. "Here comes the groom!"

Jamie shook his head, but laughed. "Tone it down, Annetta. Tone it down, please."

I reached for his hand, but Annetta dropped back, was suddenly between us.

"How long will you stay?" she demanded. "Forever, Jamie? Say it'll be forever."

"You talk as if you're ten years old." He grinned. "When are you going to grow up?"

The soft drawl that I had noticed for the first time when we arrived had become stronger.

"Cute," Annetta said. "But I notice you haven't told me."

"How can I tell you how long we'll be here when I don't know myself?" Jamie answered. He went on, "Besides, you won't be here forever yourself. One of these days, a knight on a white charger will come prancing up from town, and he'll carry you away."

"Oh, quit it," Annetta said scornfully. "I'm not fifteen any more. And I don't want a knight on a white charger. I don't want anybody, and I don't want to go away. I just want all of us, here, together, the way it used to be."

She thrust open wide carved doors, and flipped a switch. I caught my breath at the sight of the huge room. Two big chandeliers, bulbs shaded by pink crystal, hung from the high ceiling. Deep sofas fronted a large fireplace on one wall. Floor-to-ceiling windows were draped in wine velvet that harmonized with thick Oriental rugs.

I paused to look, filled with strange awe. I could hardly believe that real people lived among such beautiful things; that they took for granted the small carved tables of gleaming mahogany, the polished copper.

"It's lovely," I breathed.

"Come on," Annetta said. "I'll give you the grand tour tomorrow." Then, hurrying before us: "It's been awful since you left, Jamie. First Michael, and then you," she went on in a petulant voice. "And Sebastian sick, and Henley sneaking around all the time—" She must have caught the look I sent Jamie, for she giggled, cried, "Oh, Jamie, I'll bet you dragged Bobby in here just plain cold, didn't you? You didn't tell her about me, or Michael, or any of us."

I flinched when she called me "Bobby." "Robin" was my name. I didn't like being called by any other. It made me feel as if, in coming to Cromwell Crossing, I had surrendered my own identity, had become someone else. The thought made me shiver, and the rose-colored lights seemed to dim. I waited hopefully for Jamie to tell Annetta to address me as "Robin."

Instead, he grinned. "Guilty as charged," Jamie said. "I was afraid if I warned her about you, Annetta, she wouldn't marry me at all."

Annetta ignored that. She turned to me, black eyes quickly sparkling. "Michael's the brother, the oldest— and does he take that seriously! He always has. Being Sebastian's right hand, and running Jamie and me as if —as if we were kids. *His* kids." Her mouth drooped in a pout. She turned away again, went ahead of us, leading the way through a darkened room that appeared to be a formal dining area.

I was beginning to accustom myself to her swift changes of mood, to realize that Annetta was an eighteen-year-old, somewhat immature who had probably been alone too much, and who had had little feminine companionship. I was twenty-three, not so long from being eighteen myself that I had forgotten what it was like. Though my life had been completely different from Annetta's, I could guess a little of what she felt.

It didn't surprise me when Annetta burst into a triumphant: "Here comes the bride! Here comes the groom!" and singing, bowed us with a flourish through the door.

The kitchen was a big room, one wall covered by a large stone fireplace surrounded by shining copper pots. A large round table filled a corner. A brace of potted plants made a garden under a wide window.

A small dumpy woman turned from the laden table. "Jamie! You!"

She stood very still, plainly waiting, until he flung himself toward her; then her arms came up to hold him tight, and her dark face became radiant with love.

Jamie, grinning, said, "You heard the song, Maria. Now don't start pretending that you don't know what it means. This is my wife; this is Robin."

"You! Married!" she exclaimed. She looked directly at me for the first time.

Annetta murmured, "Maria's our Indian. She's been with us forever and ever. You'll have to work to win *her*."

Annetta's words registered on my mind, but I didn't respond to them.

For Maria, the look of love gone, was staring at me. Pain, fright, seemed to touch her eyes and mouth so briefly that I wondered if I had seen it at all. The expression was there, then gone, leaving her face blank. Maria stared at me as if I were some foreign object, a strange animal perhaps, some unwanted small nothing which had wandered into her kitchen.

Maria had slanted black eyes set above high round cheeks, a broad mouth under a small wide nose. Her

Indian skin was dusky. Her hair was black and straight, parted at the center and drawn into two thick braids that hung, tied with small blue ribbons, over her shoulders. A loose blouse, a full pleated skirt, made her shapeless, but her feet were tiny in pale-blue buckskin boots. I knew that she was an old woman, but I knew as well that she was ageless.

I held myself still under her scrutiny. It seemed as if Maria stared at me, looked into my eyes, into my soul, for immeasurable time. Then she came forward. She took my face between her work-scored hands. She touched my cheeks, her black eyes still somber. Finally, her broad mouth moved in a smile.

"Jamie's wife," she said.

If there had been pain and fright in her eyes before, it was gone now. Instead, there was acceptance, even joy. I didn't know why, but I felt as if she were making me a promise when she repeated, "Jamie's wife."

"Robin," Jamie said, the sound of his voice breaking a spell I hadn't known was upon me until it was gone.

"I call her 'Bobby,' " Annetta said.

Maria's hands dropped from my cheeks, removing their warmth. She turned to look at Annetta. Slowly she shook her head. "No, Annetta. This is 'Robin,' and it suits her well. Small, gentle Robin—like the bird."

I didn't see Annetta's reaction because, when Maria spoke to her, something inside me seemed to whisper in almost audible words, "No, Maria, don't be good to me. Don't trust me. Don't call me gentle."

Annetta interrupted my trembling thoughts by asking, "And where's Henley? Sebastian wants champagne."

"I've been here, waiting my turn," the voice came from behind me.

Startled, I looked around. I hadn't heard anyone come in. But Henley was there, smiling gently. He was small, narrow-shouldered, thin. His rimless glasses reflected the light hiding his eyes. He looked very much like the head bookkeeper at Greenley's, a wholesale outlet, where I had modeled coats years before.

Henley offered his hand. I took his small dry fingers into mine, and thanked him for his best wishes in a tremulous voice, sounding for all the world like a bride overcome by happiness.

That, too, was good. I thought that no one but myself could realize what was happening to me. No one knew that the burden of make-believe had become too heavy for me to bear. But Jamie's arm slid around my waist, fingers clenching painfully into my flesh, bracing me.

As he held me, Jamie greeted Henley. Then he said apologetically, "Listen, excuse us, will you? It's been a long trip. We're pretty tired." And, to Maria, "My rooms?"

"Oh, yes," she said. "They are all ready for you."

It was then, for the first time, that I noticed how carefully she spoke. As if the words were not quite comfortable on her tongue. As if she had known another language before she learned English, and still had to make a mental translation from one to another.

"You heard about the champagne?" Jamie asked.

"Chilling," Henley assured him.

"Then give us half an hour. We'll get the travel dust off and come down."

Jamie turned me toward the door. Unwillingly, I paused to look back to smile.

Maria was watching me, dark eyes somber, her hands twisting themselves together. Henley politely returned my smile. Annetta tossed her head; the diamonds at her ears twinkled and danced.

I let Jamie push me before him under the rose chandeliers through the dark dining room into the main hall. I shivered inside, knowing that something was wrong. Something was wrong at Cromwell Crossing.

Jamie thrust me toward the stairs, his arm still around my waist as if he didn't trust me to follow him; he was again showing that odd sensitivity to my feelings that I had noticed before. Because I *didn't* want to follow him. I wanted to escape his encircling arm and to run for the entrance door and for the freedom of the trees outside.

But I didn't run. Together, we climbed the steep flight in silence.

The two staircases ended at opposite walls. Their mahogany banisters formed a perfect oval balcony around an open well. From the cathedral ceiling above it, another elaborate rose-crystal chandelier was suspended. A line of doors opened on a hallway in the north wing over which I knew Sebastian's rooms were located.

Jamie, fingers still pinching the flesh at my waist, led me to the opposite wing. He pushed a door open, pressed me ahead of him, as he turned on a light.

I had a quick impression of a large comfortable sitting room, and, beyond it, a lamplit bedroom. One part of my mind noticed the surroundings, considered how convenient the suite could be, even recorded the three stacked bags that had been brought up from the car. Another part of my mind was flooded with misgivings.

As Jamie closed the door gently behind us, I asked, hearing the hoarseness in my voice, "Why didn't you tell me? Your father's a sick old man, Jamie. Didn't you know?"

"What's wrong with you, Robin?" Jamie countered.

"But you should have told me!"

"About Sebastian? Why? What difference does it make?"

I couldn't answer. I didn't know myself why it mattered. But I knew it did.

Jamie went on. "Sebastian's a tough old bird. He had

a heart attack a year ago. But you don't know him. He'll hang on. He and Michael—that good right hand of his. Two cut from the same cloth. Not like me. I'm different from them. Ask them and they'll tell you. They won't mince words. Wait until old Sebastian gets started. I'm different; I always have been. So I'm not going to wait. I want what's coming to me *now*. Now, when I'm young and can enjoy it. I'm not going to wait like a vulture until old Sebastian finally dies. Michael's got his, and I want mine. No matter what Sebastian says."

The boyish look was gone from Jamie's face. His pale-blue eyes were hot. The quick hungry impatience in him cut lines on his brow, put grooves in his cheeks. He was suddenly older than twenty-four. He was as old as greed, as old as evil itself.

I closed my eyes and turned away, knowing if he were evil, then I also was evil.

"Nobody's going to stop me, Robin," Jamie went on. "You're here to help me. Remember that!"

Chapter *THREE*

I HAD unpacked my bag and hung my clothes away. I could sense Jamie's watching relief as I settled in.

Finally, Jamie said, "It's not as if we're hurting anybody."

I couldn't see that we would be hurting anybody either; however, something inside me felt sickened and afraid. I said briefly, "I'll change now, Jamie. Maybe you had better get dressed too."

He retreated to the front room. I heard him open his bags, and called, "You'd better bring that stuff in here."

"Later," he answered.

I gave myself a quick wry smile in the mirror. Old Sebastian had done his job well. Jamie was a gentleman clear through to the bone.

I washed quickly, gave my hair a few fast brush strokes. As I leaned close to my reflection to etch red on my lips, my eyes stared back at me bright and expectant behind their thick lashes.

Suddenly, I understood what I had felt in the house. I understood the sensation I'd had from the moment I saw Cromwell Crossing crouched on its craggy shelf at the edge of the world. Those demon eyes flashing at me from the blank windows, those thick waves of melancholy that flowed at me from the dark house, had been nothing more than echoes, projections of my own guilt. Of my guilt, and Jamie's.

I frowned at myself, turning away from the mirror, and trying to turn away from my disconcerting thought as well.

Jamie was right when he said we wouldn't be hurting anybody. Furthermore, if we were successful, I'd have what I'd always wanted.

But I found as I took a pale green cotton shift from its padded hanger that my hands were shaking. I clenched my fingers into fists, held them hard and tight. It was a trick, taught me by a girl at Greenley's, to break down a model's preshow stage fright. It worked for me then, and it worked for me now. My hands relaxed and steadied as I slipped into the dress, fastened the zipper.

"Okay, Jamie," I called.

He came in, carrying his clothes. "I won't be long," he told me, and went into the bathroom.

I sat on the long green chaise near the window. While I waited for him, my thoughts went back to the night just a little more than three weeks before, when it had all started.

I'd been at a party with an out-of-town buyer. It was part of my job to be nice to such men, but not "too nice." I knew, after a little while with the customer that I was going to have a more-than-ordinary problem when it came time to say good night. A lot of liquor was flowing, a lot of the sort of talk I didn't relish. I had developed a convenient headache and made such a quick convincingly sweet apology that I hoped my buyer escort would be regretful rather than angry.

Outside, it was warm, smoggy, but I drew deep relieved breaths as I waited for the hotel doorman to call me a cab.

I noticed a man leaning against the wall in the shadows. He moved, and I swung quickly away. I'd had more than enough of drunks at the party inside.

But the man was beside me, wavering on unsteady feet. "Listen, honey," he said. "I'm in trouble. Can you help me? I need a dollar to get home on. You can afford a dollar, can't you?"

I looked him up and down. He was well-dressed, although disheveled. His sandy hair was tousled, his shadowed eyes glazed. He rubbed his mouth with a trembling hand.

"I came down from 'Frisco on a party, and look——"

He turned his pockets inside out. "Not a dime. Nothing. You know how you can't get a lift these days. So how about it, honey? Want to give me a break?"

"You can't get back to San Francisco on a dollar," I told him. "Any money I give you now will go from my hand to yours and then over the bar inside the hotel."

His mouth spread in a drunken grin. "Say, honey, you've got a brain under that pretty red hair."

At that moment, the doorman came out. He looked first at me then at the grinning man beside me. He said, "The cab's on the way." After a pause, he asked, "You being bothered, miss?"

All I had to do was answer *yes* and turn my back while the grinning drunk was hustled down the block. But, somehow, I couldn't. I shook my head negatively at the doorman, and, to my relief, the cab pulled up. The doorman opened the door; I tipped him and got in. Then I looked out. The tall, sandy-haired boy—that's what he was, just a boy—was watching me, the drunken smile gone now.

"Come on," I said. "Get in."

He gave me a dazed wide-eyed look and tumbled to the seat beside me.

That was how I met Jamie Cromwell. That was how, on the strength of a crazy impulse, I took him home with me.

"Home" was a one-room apartment: sofa for bed, two secondhand chairs, hot plate for stove, dresser, bookcase, and dime-store curtains at the single window. It wasn't much, but it was the best I could afford.

I managed to get Jamie up the two flights of stairs. At my door, he protested. "Say, wait a minute, honey. Where's this?"

"This is where you pour down a gallon of coffee."

"Thank you," he mumbled.

Inside, he fell on the sofa; he collapsed there as if he were dead. It didn't take me long to make a pot of strong black coffee, but I couldn't awaken him. Sighing, because I knew that his deep sleep would last through the night, I threw a spread over him, and curled up in a chair to wait.

It was an odd thing for me, especially for me, to have done. Auburn hair and green eyes notwithstanding, I'd always been a bit timid. Life had fashioned me that way, and the same timidity had made my life more difficult. As long as I could remember, I'd been scared.

My mother had gone from the Salinas Valley to San Diego just after the beginning of World War II. She found a job in an aircraft factory, and she must have had a pretty good time until she fell in love with a redheaded sailor. A redheaded *married* sailor. When he was shipped out, she went back home, pregnant with me.

I can see now that it must have been hard on her. I was a living reminder of the mistake she'd made. A mistake her family never let her forget. I was moved back and forth between two of her brothers' homes, unwanted, unloved, wearing third-time-around hand-me-downs—too confused to fit in anywhere.

Slowly my fear built up, and, by the time I was twelve, it became rage and rebellion. I ran away and was brought back so many times that my uncles gave up on me. They pooled their meager resources and enrolled me in a small boarding school that had been established specifically for children that nobody wanted. There, I learned to cook, and sew, and to understand the deep emotional need I had for pretty things; for a home of my own; and, most of all, for security.

I finished school when I was nearly eighteen. Los Angeles was the city closest, so I looked there for work. It wasn't easy to find. My few dollars were almost gone. I was terribly afraid I would have to ask my uncles for help when a girl in the house where I roomed told me about the modeling job at Greenley's and took me to see the supervisor.

The department head hired me even though I was shaking so badly I could barely walk across the floor for her. The pay wasn't much, but at least I could manage.

I stayed for three years; then I took the job I now had because it offered a bit more money. I just barely supported myself, buying clothes at wholesale prices, eating my meals in drugstores. I had a tiny emergency savings account, my bits of secondhand furniture—and that was all.

But I wanted all the bright beautiful things the world had to offer. I wanted them with the deep passionate hunger of the coward who knows he will never have the strength to make his dreams come true.

That was how it was with me the night I followed a crazy impulse and brought Jamie Cromwell home with me.

My visitor slept through the night while I dozed in my chair. He awakened, squinted against the dim sun in the room and held his head forlornly. He took the aspirin and coffee I gave him.

Finally, haggard and bewildered, he said, "Honey, I guess you better tell me who you are, and where I am, and what I've done now."

The curious blend of loneliness and pity that had made me want to help him the night before was gone.

I told him, "The first thing I've got to say is— I don't like to be called 'honey.' My name is Robin."

He gave me an open boyish smile. "Good. I will comply with your wish."

"You're in my apartment," I went on. "You were so drunk on the street outside the Commodore Hotel that I was afraid you'd get into trouble. So I brought you here to sober you up. You passed out on me instead."

"You mean you never saw me before? And you did that?"

I nodded agreement.

"That's the wildest thing I ever heard," he said wonderingly.

"Maybe it was the good story you handed me. You said you'd come down from San Francisco on a party and didn't have any money to get home."

He grinned. "That's true enough. I remember that part. I just don't remember running into you."

"You weren't in particularly good condition."

The man grinned again. "You sound extremely disapproving, Robin."

"I am. I don't see why a boy like you should get so drunk he ends up panhandling."

He groaned. "Save me the lectures. I've had them all —in every variation."

"They didn't help much."

"Why should they? I never listened."

"But—panhandling," I protested.

He laughed. "What's wrong with it?"

"If you don't know, then I can't tell you."

I was beginning to wish I hadn't followed my wild impulse. This man hardly seemed worth missing a night's sleep for.

"I'd do anything to get what I wanted," he said bluntly.

He was telling me the literal truth, but I didn't believe him. He ran his hands through his sandy hair, then gave me a boyish smile, his wide-spaced blue eyes shining.

"But you," he went on, "I just don't figure you, Robin. Why did you bother with me? Really. What did you think you'd get out of it?"

I shrugged. "Nothing."

"Nobody does anything for nothing."

"Now you know different."

He leaned back on the sofa, eyeing me speculatively. "Now I know," he agreed. Then, "Little, redheaded, green-eyed, shapely. Hmmmm——"

"Since you've completed the inventory, you could think about starting for home," I told him.

My visitor just looked at me for a short while, silent,

thoughtful. Then he said, "Listen, Robin. I've got a great idea. Why don't you marry me?"

"You must still be drunk."

"No. I'm stone-cold sober. But it's plain I need somebody to take care of me, and you seem very fit for the job, so why——"

I poured another cup of coffee, put it into his hand. "I'm peculiar. I like to be introduced to men before I marry them."

He laughed and introduced himself. "I'm Jamie Cromwell." Then, very seriously, he repeated the proposal.

Just as seriously, I said, "No, but thank you."

A little later, Jamie left, refusing the money I offered him. I never expected to see him again. But, that evening, he was back, a huge bunch of roses under his arm. He explained that he'd borrowed money from a Los Angeles friend and he had located the car he'd left in a parking lot. He now wanted to take me to dinner to prove he wasn't a disreputable lout.

I was impressed with his convertible and with his easy assurance. But, when Jamie told me over flickering candlelight that he'd fallen in love with me at first sight, and wanted me to marry him before he left for San Francisco the next morning, I just laughed. He didn't pursue the subject, and we had a good time together. Then he disappeared for a few days, and I thought my adventure with Jamie Cromwell was over.

One evening, however, he was waiting for me outside the showroom when I left work.

"You didn't think you'd gotten rid of me, did you?" Jamie grinned charmingly. "I went back for some clothes and a bank roll, that's all."

I saw my suitor almost every night for the next three weeks. Though I learned very little about him, I soon realized that his boyish charm covered a core of bitterness.

Each time we were together, Jamie asked me to marry him, and, each time, I said I wouldn't.

Then, one night, when we'd come back to my room, Jamie asked, "Okay, Robin, then tell me what's wrong with me?"

"Nothing, Jamie." I curled up in my chair. "But you're not in love with me, and I'm not in love with you. That's what's wrong."

He looked at me and grinned. "Is it because you think I'm a drunk? You ought to know by now I'm not. It was just that one time——"

"You're trying to con me, Jamie. I know that much. I don't know why, or what you expect to gain from me, but this isn't a real courtship."

He was quiet for a long time before he said gently, "I should have known better. You're right, Robin. I *am* trying to con you."

That was when he told me about the money in the Cromwell family, about his father's old-fashioned ideas.

"Old Sebastian, with all he's got socked away, keeps me on an allowance, so much the month. Me, twenty-four years old, and I have to account for every nickel I spend. I came out here three months ago because I couldn't stand living there with him any more, listening to the lectures, the reminders about how great the Cromwells have always been. They made it, so I don't have to worry. I want to live out here, up in 'Frisco, and I need money to do it."

"Then why don't you go to work and make it? That's what most people do, Jamie."

"Why should I?" he demanded. "It's all there, waiting for me. Why should I work when I don't have to?"

"Because that's what people do, I guess."

"Not this people." He grinned at me. "And this is where you come in, Robin. I'm going to level with you now. When I get married, I'm sure my father will make a settlement on me. It will be more than enough of what it will take for both of us to be happy. Little Jamie's just got to prove that he's a responsible type. A married responsible type."

"You don't need me," I said slowly. "There must be plenty of girls who'd——"

"Sure," Jamie retorted. "But the wrong kind, Robin. Old Sebastian is sharp. He's been around. If I come home with a gold digger, he'll say 'No, no, no,' until doomsday. Besides, I have to be able to trust the girl myself. After I get the money, we could wait a little while, then get a divorce. I have to be sure I won't get held up."

"What makes you think you can trust me, Jamie?"

"I can," he said. "And you can trust me too, Robin. We don't have to make this a real thing, you know. I won't take advantage. It would be strictly a money deal. For both of us. We'd go out there, to Cromwell Crossing, visit for a while, and give old Sebastian a chance to look you over. As soon as we get the settlement, we could come back here."

I shook my head. "No, Jamie."

He looked around the room. "You like living like this? There's nothing in the world you want?"

"Only everything."

Bright images flickered and faded in my mind. Closets full of clothes, planes swooping in over foreign cities . . . The Ginza in Tokyo, Montmartre in Paris, Soho in London.

Jamie got up. "Then think on it, Robin."

I didn't sleep that night. I looked at my bank book. I had fifty dollars in savings. I wandered about the room, touching the mended places in the worn furniture. I had nothing behind me, and nothing better ahead. But, after a few short weeks of deception, I would have everything that money could buy.

I told myself that, for once in my life, I would not be

a coward. I had to fight for what I wanted. I had to follow through on the lucky impulse that had led me to bring Jamie home with me. I would go along with his plan. But with one exception. I wouldn't really marry him. I couldn't force myself to make a blasphemy of wedding vows.

The next morning, I told Jamie. He protested, "But marrying me is *your* protection. Suppose I get the money and then just say, 'Thanks a lot,' and kiss you good-by?"

"I can trust you," I said, and then smiled. "Besides, I could always tell your father, couldn't I?"

Jamie nodded. "Yes, you're right. You could do that. And, actually, unless he got suspicious, he wouldn't check up."

"If your father got suspicious, it would be all over anyhow, wouldn't it?"

Jamie grinned, put out his hand. "Agreed then? You'll be the sometime Mrs. Cromwell?"

We shook on our agreement, like master criminals forming a syndicate.

The next day I paid an additional month's rent on the apartment just to be sure I'd have some place to come back to, and Jamie and I started for Cromwell Crossing. . . .

I jerked my head up. I thought I'd heard a sound. The drapes billowed in, nearly touching the chaise. I got up and went to the floor-to-ceiling window. I stepped through it onto a balcony that ran the entire length of the wing. A row of windows opened on it, some alight, some dark. A shadow moved near one of them. I stared at it, suddenly tense, then realized it was only drapery moved by the night wind. I went to the waist-high balustrade. It was lined with potted plants like those which had been in the main hall below. But up here the planters were stone.

I looked beyond the woods into the valley, now dark as a shadowed sea. Faintly, far below, I saw the glimmer of red lights which were probably the neon signs of the village.

I was wishing Jamie would hurry when I heard him call, so I went in. He was freshly shaved, carefully dressed in a light suit. A pale-blue tie matched his eyes.

"Ready?" he asked.

I nodded, and started ahead of him. But, in the sitting room, I stopped abruptly. I sat on the chaise and looked up at him. "Jamie, I'm not—I can't—go down there. Not unless you tell me some things first. I have to be prepared." He frowned at me, and I hurried on, "Besides, husbands *do* tell their wives about family stuff. If you don't get me straightened out now, I'll probably make some terrible mistake."

Jamie stood before me, sullen, impatient, silent. Finally, shrugging, he said, "It's just that I hate talking about it. Sebastian filled me to the eyeteeth with the Cromwells. But, okay, what do you want to know?"

I hesitated, not knowing where to start; then I plunged in. "There's just the three of you, right? You, your brother Michael, and Annetta?"

"Add old Sebastian and you've got the living Cromwells."

"The living Cromwells?"

Jamie shrugged again. "The ancestors are dead, you know, though too much with us." He paused, then added softly, "And my mother, too."

"Where does Michael live?" I asked quickly. "Annetta said he'd moved away a year ago."

"He's in Austin now. He handles Sebastian's business mostly from there, and his own business, too, of course. I told you our Michael's an eager beaver."

"Is he married, Jamie?"

"How long is this inquisition going on, Madam Cross-Examiner?"

"I have to know, Jamie."

"Michael was married. Sebastian gave him a whopping big pile." Jamie grinned. "That's what gave me the idea, you know."

"You said 'was married.' Is he divorced now? Did that enhance your idea?"

"Ayren, his wife, died in an accident," Jamie said shortly. "Michael was hurt too. He still has the limp."

I let that go. "And Annetta? She always lives here?"

"Sure. She went away to school a couple of times, but always got bounced back home, like me, as a matter of fact—which is what she wanted anyhow."

"Does Maria run this large house by herself?"

"She used to have a girl in from town to help when we were all at home. I guess now, between her and Henley, they can manage."

"You mean Henley's a servant?" I was bewildered. The man had seemed to move with extraordinary familiarity throughout the house.

"Not exactly, Robin. Henley works for my father, but he's a friend. An old one, like Uncle Ned Robard. Henley used to be down in Galveston, but about seven or eight years ago, he got hurt somehow or other, and he came up here to mend. He's been here ever since." Jamie chuckled. "And lucky for me! He has got me out of more trouble here and there. Without him, Sebastian would have had my head a dozen times."

I could think of only one more question. I wanted to ask Jamie (but I didn't) why he returned bitterness for his family's love.

I got up, smoothing my dress. "Let's go down, Jamie."

"Just concentrate on what you're going to get out of this, and you'll do all right," Jamie told me.

"On what we'll both get out of it," I retorted.

As I went before him down the steep flight of stairs, I thought how odd it was that Jamie, from having too much, and that I, from having too little, should both want the same thing.

Chapter *FOUR*

WE WERE in Sebastian's study. The enormous desk had been spread with Jamie's home-coming supper. There were tiny sandwiches, black olives, cherry tomatoes, stuffed celery, and a huge roast beef. Maria, I knew, must have been preparing the food since Jamie's call the day before announcing that he was coming home—but not announcing his marriage.

Sebastian lounged in a big black leather chair, fondling an unlit pipe in his big hand. Annetta sat at his knee, her head dipped, black curls falling over her white forehead.

Jamie and I were close in a corner of the sofa, so close that I wondered if he held me near him to gain courage from me, or simply because he didn't trust me any more. The thought made me smile. It was true I had misgivings, but I had more to lose than he did, much more.

Henley was near the spacious desk, studying the food intently as if checking off each platter against a mental list.

Sebastian said, "I phoned the Robards, and, you know Belinda, Jamie, full of the usual get-up-and-go. She promised to drag old Ned out. They should be here in a little while."

"You're making a real party." Jamie grinned. And to me, he said, "You'll like them, Robin. Aunt Belinda's your sort."

"I believe we could have champagne while we're waiting for them." Sebastian looked at Henley. "Would you call Maria in? I'd like her to drink with us." As Henley, nodding, went out, moving as quietly as a cat on velvet, Sebastian continued, "Maria's been with us since I first married. She came down from the north with my wife, you know." He touched Annetta's black curls. "She loves the children. And especially this one. This one is still her baby."

"Too much baby," Annetta retorted. "I'm getting too old to have a nursemaid follow me around."

"Follow you around?" Jamie jibed. "Fat chance! Nobody could keep up with you." He turned to me. "If you want a guide, Annetta's the best bet. She knows the country like nobody else."

"Do you like caves, Bobby?" Annetta demanded eagerly. "There are wonderful ones up the mountain. I'd love to show them to you."

Henley silently crossed the rug. Maria came in behind him and stood near Annetta. She gave the girl a disapproving look, a light touch on her white cheek. But the slightly accented words she spoke were gentle.

"You are a big girl now, Annetta. You must not climb in the caves."

I didn't think that I would particularly enjoy scrambling around inside the mountain, but I couldn't reject Annetta's first offer of friendship so I said quickly, "Why, Annetta, that sounds like fun."

"Then you'll go with me? Tomorrow?"

"Not tomorrow. Tomorrow, Robin must rest," Maria put in. "She has come a long way."

"But some time," Annetta persisted.

"Of course," I assured her.

Henley had partially drawn the cork from a bottle of champagne. The cork flew out with a loud popping sound, and Annetta laughed, jumping to her feet.

"A toast," she cried. "We need a toast to the new Mrs. Cromwell."

Henley filled the glasses with sparkling wine, passed them around.

"We drink to you, Robin, and to you, Jamie. Long life, and work, and love," Sebastian said in a deep quiet voice.

After they had drunk, I held the glass to my lips, suddenly choked up, unable to swallow. My eyes stung. A toast like that should be for a real marriage, I thought, not for a mockery. I looked away from Sebastian's craggy face, and caught a glimpse of Maria before I dropped my gaze to the rug. One of her wrinkled hands rested lightly on Annetta's elbow, the other held her glass. I saw a tremor on her lips, a tinge of fear in her eyes, as she drank.

"To Robin, and to Jamie," Henley said, breaking the silence.

"Who both thank you," Jamie answered.

Finally, finding my voice, I said, "Oh, yes, yes; thank you."

Maria, leaving the room, smiled at me; then at Jamie. And seeing that, I wondered if I had imagined the somber look she had given me before.

When she had gone, Sebastian said, "I called Michael, too. I knew he'd want to know."

"And how's old Michael?" Jamie asked.

"Didn't you write to him? He'd have been glad to hear from you," Sebastian answered.

"I was getting enough in the way of lectures from you yourself," Jamie told him.

Sebastian sighed, and Annetta, at his feet again, stirred.

"Two brothers—you should be closer." Sebastian looked at me, and I knew from that look, cautious, questioning though kind, that the inquisition was about to begin. But he said, "I hope you had family to stand up with you when you married, Robin."

"There's practically no one left, you know. Just two uncles in the Salinas Valley, and I knew they couldn't come, so——"

"Well, then, I wish Jamie had let us know——"

"We wanted it to be a surprise," Jamie said lazily, his boyish smile open and free. His lean body seemed relaxed against me. The nagging impatience was gone. I wondered uncomfortably if I would ever know which was the real Jamie.

"Have you lived in San Francisco long?" Sebastian asked.

"In Los Angeles," I corrected him. "For about five years. Jamie and I met there actually—at a party."

"And it clicked, and that was it," Jamie put in. "We met a month ago, and tied the knot the day before yesterday."

I touched the gold ring on my finger. The "day before yesterday" had been when I had suddenly realized that I would need one, and made Jamie stop to buy it for me.

"Tell me, what did you do in Los Angeles?" Sebastian asked, looking at me.

"I'm a model—oh, not the glamorous, high-fashion kind. I just walked around in clothes for buyers in a manufacturers' outlet." I went on quickly, "I guess I never was trained to do very much you see."

I didn't wait for any more questions. I picked and chose among the true facts of my background, telling him what I thought he wanted to know. I ended up by saying, "So, after I finished school, I went to Los Angeles, and I've been on my own ever since."

Sebastian looked pleased. "I believe in work." And, turning to Jamie, he asked. "What about you? What did you do those three months in San Francisco, boy?"

Jamie grinned. "You know what I did. Nothing."

"But it's different now," Sebastian said. "You're a married man."

I felt Jamie go taut, and leaned against him warningly.

Sebastian went on. "You could work with me here, which is what I would like, having you and Robin stay. Or, if you wanted, you could go down to Austin with Michael. You'd find a place for yourself in Cromwell affairs."

"How could I?" Jamie demanded. "I never have before."

"That was up to you." Sebastian leaned back, closed his eyes tiredly. "You could do what the rest of us have done."

My heart sank. It was obvious to me from Sebastian's words that the last thing on his mind was making the same kind of settlement on Jamie that he had made on Michael. I wondered why. But, in a moment, I understood.

Sebastian said, "You've got to prove yourself, Jamie."

I wasn't the only one on trial then. Jamie was, as well.

I pressed my fingers against his thigh, warning him not to answer.

Sebastian straightened, opened his eyes. He smiled at me. "Maybe I'm an old-fashioned man," he said. "But that's how it is, girl. My family means a lot to me. My grandfather, Michael Cromwell, walked out of South Carolina and into Texas wearing a tattered gray uniform. He had nothing but that uniform, and broken boots, and a gun. In a few years, he had himself a fine herd of cattle, and, never mind how he got it, except that about the time he sold it, he thought it would be a good idea to move on. So he came out here, put up the ferry sign, and did pretty well—for himself and for us. My father built this house, and built up our business interests, too. In my own way," he said contentedly, "I kept it going. I guess all of us Cromwells have made our mark one way or another. There's a bit of the buccaneer in all of us, and we've used it when we needed it."

"Oh, Sebastian," Annetta interrupted, "she doesn't want to hear about all that old, old stuff. Why don't you tell her about Galveston?"

Sebastian laughed. "Maybe I will. Maybe, one of these days, I'll just do that."

"But why not now?" Annetta insisted.

"Because there's a time and a place for everything. And this isn't the time," Sebastian answered. "I'm talking about the family. It's natural, when a man realizes he is old, to look back and to look ahead, too. I'm not the man I was. I need new legs, and, sometimes, I think I need new brains. I can't have those, but I can have something better. Sons to be my legs and brains, and their sons to help them when the time comes." He sighed. "I want to see the future. When Michael married Ayren, I thought I saw the beginning of it. Then Ayren was killed right here on Cromwell lands, and Michael's unborn child was killed with her. I couldn't believe it had happened, and my heart tore itself trying not to believe."

I saw Annetta snuggle her head to Sebastian's thigh. Her hand closed over his, held it.

Her father glanced down at her, but then his eyes came up to Jamie and me again, and he went on. Michael's not the man he was, perhaps never will be any more. There's only you, Jamie—you and Robin now to carry on the Cromwell name."

I looked into Sebastian's sad tired eyes and I knew then that only Jamie was being tested. Sebastian had accepted me. He would have accepted any presentable girl that Jamie brought home. I was sorry, sorry I had come.

I wished I could think of the right words for an answer. But there were no appropriate words.

Then Henley said quietly, "I believe I hear the Robards' car."

Ned Robard bounded into the room like a lamb herded to the fold by a collie. He was small, hardly taller than I, and wiry. His head was as bald and shiny as a hard-boiled egg, and his face was strangely askew, with too much jaw and not enough temple. Belinda Robard was tall, shaped by an old-fahioned corset at bosom and hip. Her short gray hair was crimped into neat waves under a net. Her face was round and pink and excited. For all her size, she moved quickly at her husband's heels, talking all the while in a high breathless voice.

"This is wonderful!" she cried. "Annetta, Sebastian, Henley, just look, we're all together again. I'm so happy I could weep. Let me get my fill of you, Jamie, and there's the Robin I've heard about."

I rose; and so did Jamie.

Belinda reached him, seized him, spun him around and kissed him, just a fraction of a moment before Ned did the same. There was a confusion of glad exclamations, and introductions.

Belinda, holding me at arm's length, said without sounding patronizing, "My, you're a little one. You're the littlest bride ever brought to this house."

"And you're a sight for sore eyes, boy," Ned told Jamie, a smile twisting his askew face. "We've missed you, that we have."

"So much," Belinda said. "So much we even forgive you for not writing."

Henley passed full champagne glasses around, and urged us toward the food. We served ourselves. Before we sat down again, Ned sang out, "To Jamie and Robin, happy days always!" with Belinda echoing him joyfully.

Again, as Jamie and I were toasted, I felt my throat tighten.

It was so obvious that no shadow marred their pleasure in seeing Jamie, or in greeting the girl they thought to be his bride.

Belinda settled her bulk beside me, a stacked plate on her plump knees. "I'm already tipsy," she said breathlessly. "Just one sniff of a wine, and my head goes into a whirl."

"One sniff of anything liquid," Ned put in. "And that includes water," at which Belinda produced a surprisingly youthful giggle.

Sebastian leaned back, smiling a little, obviously pleased, while Annetta snuggled against his knees.

There was some general talk about people who were strangers to me, about some of Sebastian's interests in Texas, questions about Michael. Then Ned asked Jamie if we had any plans. Jamie explained that we hadn't yet decided where we would live. He went on, in an obvious diversion, relating some amusing anecdotes about our experiences on the trip with a deaf gas-station attendant, and, later, with a hobo poet.

Belinda leaned closer to me to say, "Robin, my dear, I want you to come into town, to visit with us right away. Get Jamie to bring you."

I had started to answer, to thank her, when Annetta got up, thrusting aside her untouched food. "I'm going to sleep," she announced defiantly.

For a moment, no one spoke, and then everyone spoke at the same time, saying good night too quickly.

As soon as Annetta had gone, Belinda turned to me. "Why don't we leave the men to their talk, Robin? I could do with a bit of fresh air. I get these hot flashes, and I have one now. Nothing will do me but getting out under the sky."

"Hot flashes," Ned snorted. "You got over them years ago. You only want to get Robin off by herself!"

"Mind the steps," Sebastian warned us as we went out.

"He worries," Belinda told me. "It's a crazy wonderful old house, but, like all of them, it has its booby traps. I never liked the terrace, for instance, and never will. You'll see what I mean by daylight." She led me into the main hall, then out the front door on the valley side.

We stopped on a wide stone porch. To my left, I could see the room we had just left, its long windows touching the ground level. I heard the murmur of Sebastian's voice, then Jamie's. The porch extended the full length of the south wing. I looked up and saw the balcony that ran past my bedroom window. Its arched overhang was well beyond the porch where we stood.

Belinda said, "I hope you don't mind about Annetta. She gets that way sometimes. Poor child, she can't help it. Being alone here so much. It'll be good for her to have someone her own age—well, almost her own age—even if you are a married woman."

"Annetta seems very much the individualist," I said carefully, "but she's very sweet, too."

"I'll pray you and Jamie stay here. I know you're the one who brought him back. I know you can keep him home if you try. And I'm glad, Robin. There's been so much tragedy in this house. It needs a change of luck."

"Tragedy?" I echoed.

"Jamie told you about Michael and Ayren, of course. Oh, that was terrible. Ayren was so beautiful, so young and alive. She brought sunlight into Cromwell Crossing. And she was so happy. They all were. Even Annetta, which did surprise me, because, after all, Ayren came in as a stranger and took over. Poor Annetta, she was always possessive about her men. A few days after Ned told Ayren she was expecting, she wanted to come to town for tea with me. She never liked that awful road so Michael brought her. Something went wrong with the automobile. It was an awful crash. Ayren died almost at once.

"Michael's leg was pinned underneath the car. Annetta was out on the mountain, and heard the sound of the crash; she dragged Michael out more dead than alive. Jamie found her there, screaming and hugging Michael, and he got help from town. There was nothing to do for Ayren, but Ned managed to save Michael's leg, maybe even his mind. Though he changed, poor boy. How could he help but change? We didn't realize it so much until later.

"For that night, Sebastian had the coronary that's made him so sick since. He was hardly out of danger when Michael left, cast on his leg, a new grimness in his face. He said it was because the business in Austin couldn't wait. But we all knew he just couldn't bear being here, reminded of Ayren. That was a little more than a year ago, and he's never been back."

"It was a terrible thing," I said in a shaky voice, painfully touched by Belinda's recital, knowing that she was right—Cromwell Crossing truly needed a change of luck. But I knew, too, that I couldn't bring the joy that was required to push the shadows back.

"Terrible for all of them," Belinda continued. "Poor Annetta. I'll never forget her face when Sebastian collapsed. And terrible most of all for Michael, of course. He folded into himself those first few days. I saw it happen. He was always quiet—still water running deep, I suppose. Jamie and Annetta are two of a kind, born hellions and headaches. But Michael is Sebastian over again, except with even more steel. Nothing could divert him when he set his mind. And responsible?"

Belinda's giggle suddenly rippled on the cool night air. "Michael is all the way responsible, and always was, too. Even when he was a child. I told you, different from Annetta, and from Jamie, too, Robin. I hope you won't mind that I say it. When you have your own children, you'll understand. You love each one for what he is. Not for what you want him to be. Sebastian would be a happier man tonight, and always, if he could only accept his children for what they are individually."

"I hope I remember," I said.

"You will," Belinda told me comfortably. "But there, I do think I've run on too long. My hot flash is gone— which means you must be freezing."

"It's pleasant out though."

I saw a faint smile on her shadowed face. "I am nearly as bad as a mother-in-law. And you are a dear sweet child to put up with me, Robin. I know you're dead tired, longing for bed, and wishing you hadn't heard all my rambling. Yet you are a part of this family now and should know these things even if I am turning into a talkative old woman."

"I like to talk to you," I told her sincerely, happy that I did not have to pretend. "I hope I can visit with you in town."

"Why, you shall," Belinda assured me comfortably as we went indoors.

I didn't know then how soon that visit would be.

In a few minutes, Belinda had herded Ned out to their car. Sebastian retired, while Henley and Maria cleared up the study. Jamie and I went upstairs.

I felt numb, shrunken with fatigue, but Jamie was jubilant. When we were in our suite, with the door closed, he cried, "It worked, Robin. He likes you. They all do. It's going to be okay." He strode around the room, restless with excitement.

"I think you're in for a surprise, Jamie," I said gently.

"Sebastian may have taken me at face value, but I've got an idea that, married or not, you don't get a settlement yet."

"If I don't, you don't. But I will. I won't be his little boy on a string any more," Jamie retorted. He went into the bedroom, caught up a pillow and blanket, and brought them back to the sitting room sofa. "What's the doom talk for, all of a sudden?"

"I don't know. I just feel—I guess I think you're lucky to have people who care about you."

"I'm going to be luckier, Robin. And so are you."

"It doesn't have to be this way, Jamie. You could be the son he wants you to be. He doesn't ask much of you."

Jamie laughed, a sharp bitter sound. "It's just too much for him to ask of me, Robin."

As I readied myself for bed after the door closed between us, I wondered if, somehow, the buccaneer strain Sebastian had laughed about could have been passed on. Jamie might be simply trying to get what he wanted in the usual Cromwell way.

Jamie was gone when I got up in the morning. I dressed in shorts and a sleeveless shirt and went out on the balcony. The sun was bright, making a golden bowl of the valley. A few cottony clouds drifted slowly across the endless blue sky.

By day, the plants in their heavy pots seemed to be dying for lack of water. The stone of the balustrade was stained and discolored.

A flagstone terrace, laid from the broad front steps that led to the porch beneath me, stretched out to the end of the shelf on which the house was set. At one side, the flat stones had crumbled away. The other three had a sort of natural fence, apparently the tips of close-growing spruce. I didn't understand that until later, when I'd gone to look, and saw, peering over, the sheer drop that ended where the growth of spruce ended far, far below.

The house was silent when I went downstairs. I hesitated in the main hall. Then, I decided to go to the kitchen, as I heard voices from that direction.

Maria welcomed me with a warm smile, immediately poured me coffee. Henley, catfooted as always, pulled out a chair for me. He took up a covered tray, saying, "I'll take this in to Sebastian. He always rests in the morning." He went out.

Maria told me that she'd heard Jamie drive away a few minutes before. Annetta, she went on, had gone for a morning walk.

I finished my coffee, refusing Maria's insistent plea that I eat a "real" breakfast, and went outdoors.

First, I satisfied my curiosity about the spruce-tip fence, retreating quickly from the perilous edge. Then, enjoying the warmth of the sun, I lay down on the flagstones with my face in the shade cast by the balcony above.

I don't know how long I lay there, relaxing into mindless dreaming; pretending, perhaps, that I had at last found the place where I belonged. It was a time of languor, of peace.

Suddenly, the stillness was broken by a raw grating sound. I opened my eyes. All I saw was a fleeting shadow, like the quick swoop of a bird. But some deep animal instinct moved me. I flung myself backward— under the overhanging balcony. Where I'd been lying a second before, a huge pot crashed down, flying to pieces in great jagged shards as it hit the terrace. The explosive sound it made seemed to repeat itself in long rolling echoes.

A chunk of stone, razor-sharp, had knifed into my shin. But I felt no pain. Numbed, I curled into a trembling ball. A hot slick of blood spread through my fingers.

Henley burst out of the house, Maria with him, her dusky face full of terror. Thrusting them aside to leap the steps came someone I had never seen before, yet I knew him instantly. It could only be Michael Cromwell.

Michael reached me before the rolling echoes stilled.

Time seemed to catch and hold, like a white thread on black wool, while Michael and I stared at each other. He was tall, wide-shouldered, but whipcord lean. His short-cropped black hair hugged his well-shaped head. His face was tanned and lined. Black brows angled above his startling eyes, light gray eyes that were shallow, curtained, allowing nothing of what went on behind them to come through. But they were eyes which saw, measured, judged.

Time moved again in a confusion of shouts as Michael bent over me, demanding in a low toneless voice, "Where are you hurt?"

I looked past his shoulder. Annetta, white-faced, was flinging herself down the steps; Sebastian clung to the door, and Jamie was coming onto the terrace.

Now, suddenly, as if from nowhere, they had all appeared, when only a moment before the house had been empty and still.

I shuddered, and shook my head. I couldn't answer Michael. He spoke without looking up. "Henley, you had better go up to Sebastian. Tell him it's all right. Maria, get me a cold cloth." And, to me, "Let me see."

As I let go and straightened my leg, I felt a slow throb of pain.

Jamie was beside me then asking excitedly, "What happened?"

Michael answered him. "A pot must have fallen from the balcony. She's got a bad cut. You'd better take her in to Uncle Ned's." He went on, "I'm Michael, Jamie's brother."

"Yes," I whispered. "Yes. I know." Those were the first words I had been able to say.

"Funny way for us to meet," he commented. "We'll do it more properly later on."

I was grateful for his matter-of-fact tone. I knew that the slightest sign of sympathy would have dissolved me into shivering hysterics.

Maria brought me a cold wet cloth. She knelt beside me, her lips moving. "Robin," she murmured. "Robin."

It was Michael who took the cloth from her trembling hands, who bound my cut leg; Michael who lifted me to my feet.

It was only then, as I leaned against him, still shivering, that I realized Annetta had been plucking at his shoulder all the while, touching him, demanding, "Michael, Michael, when did you come? Talk to me, Michael, tell me."

I moved free of his arms, and pain flashed—a quick hot arrow through my leg. My knees turned to water. Michael was looking at Annetta, answering her finally, but he seemed to sense my weakness; his arms were there to steady me.

"Drive her in to Uncle Ned's now," he told Jamie and waited until Jamie held me before turning away.

"I want to go upstairs first," I said.

"There's no need to, Robin."

"I have to, Jamie. I'll need a skirt."

He shrugged. "Women! You almost get yourself killed, and you're worried about what the doctor will think."

I took a slow faltering step. He steadied me, an arm at my waist, as we went inside.

Sebastian, looking gray, was waiting. "You all right, girl?" he asked shakily.

I tried to smile. "Of course, I am."

"All right enough to worry about showing Uncle Ned too much of her pretty legs," Jamie put in.

Sebastian gave me a slow relieved smile. "You've got the right kind of spine, Robin." And, then, to Michael, "I can hardly believe you're here, son. I know I haven't even said hello. But we'll get to it, now I know that Robin's all right."

Michael slid a glance at me, light eyes flashing in his tanned face, all-seeing eyes meeting mine. I felt as if he could see into me, through me, with that one expressionless glance. Leaning on Jamie, I turned to go upstairs. As I climbed slowly, wincing with effort, I heard the two deep voices blending with Annetta's excited questions. I thought I sensed that gray expressionless glance follow me.

I remembered what Belinda had said. Michael was a man with steel in him. Once he set his mind, he couldn't be diverted. He was an introverted man. I wondered why he had suddenly come back to Cromwell Crossing.

Jamie said, "That was wild. Talk about homecomings! Michael flew in this morning. He phoned the house to get Henley to drive to the field for him, but I answered and went instead. We were just pulling in when we heard the crash. By the time I had cut the motor, Michael was through the house and out on the terrace."

"Why did he come, do you suppose?"

Jamie grinned. "Now why do you think? To look you over, of course."

I nodded, too busy trying to ignore the throbbing in my leg to answer. Jamie waited in the sitting room while I hobbled into the bedroom to find my skirt, the excuse I had for coming up. Then, stumbling, I hurried out to the balcony.

I saw the empty space where the fallen planter had rested, the round stain where it had been centered on the balustrade, the freshly scratched scar that led to its rim. I touched the next pot in line. I couldn't lift it. I leaned my weight into it, pushing hard. It slid an inch or two,

and I heard the same grating sound I'd heard before—
The sound that had made me look up to catch the sight
of a swooping shadow.

I jumped back as if threatened again.

Below me, I saw Michael. He stood on the terrace, a
hand shading his eyes, watching me.

I turned to the open window.

Jamie called, "Robin, what are you doing out there?"

I had to force myself to move, reluctant to go in, for I
knew that someone in the house had wanted to see me
dead.

Chapter *FIVE*

I HESITATED, shivering. Then, finally, I made myself step
through the window. The room was dim, cold, after the
bright hot sun on the balcony.

Jamie said, "You haven't even gotten dressed yet."

"I know—I thought I'd look——"

My knees suddenly gave way. I sank down on the edge
of the green lounge.

"You thought you'd look at what?" Jamie demanded.

"The balustrade, Jamie. To see——"

He cut in, "Let's get you to town."

It was hard to put it into words. To say bluntly: "Jamie, somebody tried to kill me." I took a long slow
breath. Even then, attempting to speak calmly, I found
myself almost stammering. "But I—listen, Jamie, somebody tried——"

Again, he cut in. "You're all shook up, aren't you? Where's that spine old Sebastian was talking about? Does your leg hurt you that much?"

I had completely forgotten the cut. I looked down, saw blood staining the bandage Michael had applied. I wondered briefly what Michael had been thinking as he watched me on the balcony. But I quickly forgot him, for on seeing the blood, I felt the quick hard throb of pain.

Jamie said, "If you insist, I'll get your skirt. Otherwise, come on as you are."

I looked down at my empty hands. The skirt? What had I done with it? I remembered that I had snatched it out of the closet. "It's somewhere," I said vaguely.

"Women!" Jamie groaned.

"Maybe it's on the balcony. I guess I dropped it." Jamie started out. I stopped him. "You look, too, Jamie. There's a mark on the balustrade that shows——"

But he made an impatient sound and went out. In a moment, in too short a moment, he was back.

"Did you see it?" I asked.

"See what?" He tossed me the skirt, went on, not waiting for my answer. "Climb into that, will you?"

I took the skirt and pulled it over my head. I slid it down and buttoned it at my waist. Then I slipped my shorts out from underneath. My knees gave way again; once more I sank down on the green chaise.

Jamie grinned. "Even when all to pieces, you don't forget your modesty."

I ignored that. "But the mark, Jamie? Did you see where the pot was pushed off the balustrade?"

"What are you talking about?" he demanded. His pale-blue eyes suddenly narrowed.

"It was pushed off, Jamie. It didn't just fall."

He raised me to my feet. "It looks like you've got a good case of shock. Let's get in to Uncle Ned's, and no more stalling. Okay?"

Tears stung my eyes. My throat tightened. "But don't you understand?" I cried. "Don't you want to?"

Jamie grinned at me. "Are you sure you didn't get hit on the head, Robin? Now, calm down and we'll talk about it later."

It was ridiculous. There I stood, knowing beyond a doubt that someone had tried to kill me. Jamie's hand was on my arm, holding me so that he must feel the quick frightened trembling I still couldn't control. Yet he smiled at me and tried to dispel my terror by joking. I couldn't stop the hysterical little giggle that filtered past my quivering lips.

Jamie's fingers tightened around my arm. "Hell's bells, Robin, don't start that."

I swallowed hard, and let him lead me downstairs. I knew it was no use to try to explain the incident to him then. And I couldn't really blame him. I sounded too incoherent to be believed no matter what I said. Perhaps, driving in, I could tell him, make him understand.

But, as we came down into the main hall, Annetta bounded out of Sebastian's study slamming the door behind her. "I haven't seen Michael for a whole year," she raged, "and now they send me out as if I'm a baby. Oh, it makes me sick!"

Jamie laughed. "If you looked in a mirror, you'd know why they treat you like a baby. Your lower lip is out to here and more."

"I don't care," Annetta cried, flinging back her long dark hair. "I want to see Michael. I want to talk to him." But the pout disappeared. "Are you going to Uncle Ned's? Can I ride in with you?" Without waiting for an answer, she danced ahead to throw open the wide doors. "Yes, that's what I'll do! That'll fix Michael!"

"You could ask permission before you decide," Jamie said. "This isn't exactly a pleasure trip for Robin."

Annetta swung back. Momentarily, there was a deep

cold blankness in her face. Then she saw that Jamie was grinning. She looked at me as if she had only then realized that I was hobbling along beside him.

"Oh, Bobby," the girl cried. "Does it hurt bad? I *am* sorry. What an awful thing to happen on your first day here! I'm a savage, but, honestly, with Michael coming so suddenly, I just forgot all about it."

Shaken as I was, I noticed that Annetta still refused to call me by my own name. Once again, I waited for Jamie to remind her that my name was Robin. Once again, he didn't.

He said, "If you're coming, then come on, Annetta. We've wasted enough time. Robin's a heroine to put up with this family at all, and you're——"

But his sister didn't wait for more. She skipped down the steps, and flung herself into the back seat of the convertible. "Now," she crowed, "who's holding who up, I'd like to know?"

I let Jamie help me in.

The bright sun was blinding, the sky an impossibly brilliant blue, the red of the mountain slope behind us the color of blood. As Jamie backed away from the crouching house and swung the car toward the road, bits of sunlight flashed from the empty windows like fragments of pale fire.

I wanted to close my eyes, to shrink away into restful unconsciousness where I could forget my throbbing leg, and, even more, my fright. But, as the car sped down the swinging curves, I had to watch in terrified fascination. The beautiful sun-filled bowl of the valley disappeared; then even the sky was hidden by the thick spreading trees overhead. And, somewhere along this road, Ayren, Michael's wife, the mother of his child-to-be, had died.

I pictured Michael's still expressionless face, remembered how time had seemed to stop while we stared at each other when we first met.

Annetta's high sweet voice went on. I clenched my hands in my lap, not listening. At last, we spun past the two stone posts that marked the entrance to the grounds and swung onto the highway.

Jamie, with a sudden surprising show of concern, cut into Annetta's chatter. "Are you all right, Robin?"

I nodded, knowing that he had remembered the role he was playing.

Annetta demanded, "But what on earth happened anyway?"

"A jardiniere fell off the balcony," Jamie said, stressing the word *fell*. "It smashed right at Robin's feet. A piece of it dug a hole in her leg."

I bit back protesting words. There was no use in blurting out to Annetta what I *knew* to be true when I still hadn't convinced even Jamie.

"I always told Sebastian he should let us dump all that stuff from the conservatory out on the mountains," Annetta said virtuously. "That house is turning into one big mousetrap." And to me, "But Uncle Ned's a wonderful doctor. Don't be scared, Bobby. He'll fix your leg up good as new. You'll see. Why, I remember when——"

Her light voice went on, describing the many times Uncle Ned had healed her various wounds, and there had been many of them, with a smile and a stitch.

I repressed an involuntary shudder at her insistence on not calling me by my name and concentrated on the wide golden fields which flew by. Suddenly, the town was just ahead.

There were more houses than I had noticed in the dark the evening before. Clay-packed roads wound away from the highway. The buildings were low, box-like, made of adobe, and surrounded by bright hollyhocks. We rolled down Main Street, past the drugstore, the single café, a few gasoline stations, the post office.

"Almost there now," Jamie said, turning into a tree-lined lane, then turning again into a driveway. "The old Cromwell house, restored here and there, but mostly authentic. All four-foot thick walls of it." He chuckled. "But I'll let Aunt Belinda tell you about that. She'll love you for listening. Think you're up to it? After the excitement of this morning?"

Annetta groaned. "I'm not going to listen. Old Sebastian gives me big enough doses." She leaped from the car before it had hardly stopped, raced ahead to pound at the big door, and then pushed it open.

Jamie and I followed more slowly. By the time we reached the house, Belinda had come out to meet us, crying in her high breathless voice, "What's this Annetta's been saying about an accident?"

Belinda was wearing an old-fashioned wrap-around of blue flowers on white cotton. Even that early, her gray hair was crimped into careful waves under a gray net. Her round pink face suddenly changed, became less curious than concerned, as she slid an experienced glance over me.

"Why, Robin, dear—my goodness, child, come in. Ned's back in his office. Annetta's gone to tell him. You should have phoned—we'd have driven right out. Why, that ride down the mountain must have been awful for you——"

Still talking, she took me into her arms, held me close, at the same time guiding me through a huge white room and then across a tree-shaded patio. From cool shadow into warm sunlight . . . I squinted, pretending it was the sudden brilliance that brought tears to my eyes, rather than the comforting touch of her mothering warmth.

But she knew. She said, "Goodness, child, don't be afraid to cry if it hurts."

"It's not that bad," I mumbled. "It's just—you see, Belinda——"

Jamie, who had been silent, following us, cut in swiftly.

"Poor Robin, she had a real scare—that jar coming at her out of the blue——"

I slid a look at him, wondering if he had deliberately stopped me from blurting out my terror to Belinda. But I couldn't really tell. He was smiling boyishly, rueful but worried—the perfect picture of a concerned husband.

I was suddenly glad he had interrupted me. I needed time to think, to collect myself. It was no good to come out with wild accusations. For the first time since the black shadow had swooped towards me from the balcony, I remembered why I had come to Cromwell Crossing with Jamie. I knew that if I lost my head now, I could spoil everything. I took a long steadying breath as Belinda led me into the office.

Annetta was chanting, "And Michael came home this morning, did you hear, Aunt Belinda? Michael came home!"

Belinda cried, "Wonderful, wonderful news. And now out with you, and you too, Jamie."

They both protested, but Ned, bounding from behind his desk waved them away. "No, no. Go along you two. We don't have audiences in surgery." To me, he said, "Let's have a look." Then, like Belinda, he gave me a sharp penetrating stare and said, "Not here. I want you to lie down, Robin." He took me into a small back room, led me to a cot. "Now then—now then——"

I knew that the small wiry fingers so gently holding my wrist were actually intent on taking my pulse.

I said shakily, "It's really not so bad."

"Of course not. But let's see." He unwrapped the blood-soaked bandage, frowned, but said, "Oh, it's not so much. Just close your eyes and relax, Robin." He moved quickly at cupboard and sink. "First, a capsule. How are you on big pills? Not one of those nuts who choke, I hope." And, not waiting for an answer, "But never mind, if you are, I'll just shove it down." He was beside me again. "Here we are."

I downed the pill on a big gulp of water. When I tried to talk, he stopped me. "No, never mind. You take it easy. Let me do the worrying, and the work. Close your eyes."

I obeyed, and listened as he moved around.

He murmured, half to himself, half to me, "The capsule, down. Good. A small wash. Maybe it will sting some. Then a couple of jabs of novocain, nothing to worry about, and then some fancy hemstitching."

The antiseptic did burn. I twitched as he slid the needle into my leg the first time. But, as the novocain took hold, the hard throbbing pain disappeared. I felt myself relaxing as he had ordered. I felt myself drifting, so that even the fright was easing its grip on me.

He worked, mumbling. "Some fancy embroidery. I'll do you a fine seam. In a few months, there'll hardly be a scar. I promise you that."

I lay still, only half listening.

In a little while, the doctor said, "There. All done. And as pretty a piece for a pretty girl as I've ever done."

I opened my eyes. "Thank you, Dr. Robard."

"Dr. Robard, is it? I think it had better be 'Uncle Ned'."

"Uncle Ned," I said faintly.

"At your service." He grinned at me, rubbing his bald head to an even higher shine. "But we're not finished, you know." He raised his voice. "Belinda, out there?"

She appeared in the open doorway. "What do you think? I sent Annetta and Jamie into town."

"Good," Ned told her. "Robin, off you go to the house. Wrap yourself around a big hot cup of coffee with a small drip of brandy in it for spice, and lie down. I'll be in to see you before I send you back to the castle."

"But I'm all right now," I protested.

"Of course, you are. Only I'm the doctor. And what I say goes." He went on to Belinda. "I have to run now." He snatched up his bag, grabbed a worn straw hat from the top of the cupboard. "You see to Robin, will you? And don't let her go any place but to bed until I get back."

He patted my shoulder, blew a kiss at Belinda, and ducked around her.

"Always fast on his feet," she said comfortably. "Let's see about coffee and brandy now." Helping me off the cot, Belinda confided, "It's the funniest thing, Robin. I've been married to a doctor for thirty years, and I still hate the smell of antiseptic. You'd think——" Her voice trailed away as I stumbled. "But you couldn't care less about that right now. Does it hurt much?"

I shook my head.

"It might later. When the novocain wears off. But it shouldn't last for more than a few hours, all told, and we'll have the aspirin ready, won't we?"

I tried to smile at her, but even that small effort seemed too much for me.

Belinda steadied me, leading me back to the house. "My, that must have been a big wallop of a tranquilizer he poked into you. Robin, did you know your eyes are nearly crossed? But then, you did look so odd, you can't imagine. This way, this way——"

Her quick breathless voice went on, but I was hardly able to distinguish the words. Suddenly, I found myself lying on a soft bed, a light quilted coverlet thrown over me.

Belinda said, "There now. Comfortable? I'll be back in a minute."

Alone, I lay back with my eyes closed. The silence had a wonderful peaceful quality. I knew it was the pill that wrapped me with such sweet lassitude that I couldn't think. I was grateful for it. Later would be soon enough.

I heard voices, then Belinda saying, "No, Robin's resting."

"But Bobby's all right, isn't she?" Annetta demanded.

"Robin," Belinda said firmly. " 'Robin.' It's time you stopped the childish foolishness, Annetta. It's not polite or grown-up to give people nicknames. 'Robin' she is, 'Robin' she is called."

"Oh, all right," Annetta said sulkily. " 'Robin' then."

"She's all right," Belinda said. "But she looks as if she very nearly had the life scared out of her. Ned wants her to stay here until he gets back—a few hours at least." She added, sounding indulgent, "Jamie, you can go in for a minute."

"Then what about me?" Annetta asked.

"Listen, brat," Jamie laughed, "wait a minute and I'll buy you a soda at the drugstore."

I opened my eyes, waiting. Jamie came in. "Are you okay now?"

"It's a big fuss over nothing," I told him.

"You've made a big hit with the Robards anyhow," he whispered, grinning. "You cinched last night but good. It couldn't have been arranged better. There's nothing like being needed."

"*I* didn't arrange it," I retorted.

He shrugged, "See you later then."

Belinda came in with a tray. "Better?"

"Much," I said, starting to get up.

"Oh, no, you don't." Belinda smiled at me. "You stay snuggled into those pillows, and have a cup of coffee. Ned said 'lie down' and lie down you do."

"It's such a lot of trouble for you, and really——"

"Nonsense. I wanted you to come to see me, and you did, so there we are." Belinda handed me a full cup. "Drink it." Then she bustled around, arranging the curtains, fluffing pillows, before she settled heavily into the rocking chair near the bed. "After a bit, I'll take you on a sight-seeing trip through the house. I suppose they told you, this is the old Cromwell house. The one built when the ferry first began to pay off. True old Spanish Colonial it is. When Sebastian's father built the big house on the mountain, this was closed up. Ned and I took it over just after we were married. Thirty years ago. And very little work we had to do then or since. Except for kitchen and bathrooms, it's all just as it was made in the old days."

"What I saw when I came in looked beautiful."

"What you saw? It couldn't have been much. Why, goodness, child, you were white as a sheet when you came. You had me frightened, and that takes a lot. I've seen too much to be frightened easily. And Annetta chattering away——" Belinda's mouth suddenly fell open. "And Michael came this morning. Why, Robin, in all the excitement, I even forgot that."

"It wasn't much of a welcome for him, I'm afraid."

She frowned. "That old house—just like I said—full of booby traps. But since you're not harmed, and he's home—why, I know everything's going to be all right now." She sighed. "It will mean so much to Sebastian. And that Annetta—she'll be nearly split in two, trying to follow Jamie around, and follow Michael at the same time. Poor child, she's always been so possessive of the Cromwell men, so adoring, and demanding, and who could blame her? Since they're all she ever had. Ayren had her hands full at first, I can tell you. I'm afraid you will, too."

Remembering Annetta's insistence on calling me 'Bobby,' I asked, "Belinda, why does Annetta hate all names that begin with 'R?' "

"Rose," Belinda said softly. "Rose is her mother's name, Robin. You mustn't be offended. It is something that started a long long time ago. You see, Annetta's mother just ran off, left her here, with Sebastian. Poor

Annetta, she was only eight then. I can see her yet, screaming with nightmares. She was so afraid that Sebastian wouldn't keep her, not being her real father."

"Not her father?" I asked, bewildered. "But I thought——"

"Of course, you did. They never talk about it. Sebastian feels that he has three children, three all his. But you see, Michael and Jamie are Sebastian's sons by his first wife. She died in childbirth when Jamie was born. Dear Jamie, it was all in his mind, but he always felt they blamed him, Sebastian and Michael, that is, for his mother's death. But that's something else, isn't it? We're talking about Annetta. Yes, Sebastian, back in 1950, I guess it was, went East to Washington on business. He met Rose there. She was young, a divorcée. Annetta was a three-year-old, pretty as a picture even then. The image of her mother, she's grown to be. Sebastian married Rose, and brought her back to Cromwell Crossing, and made Annetta his daughter. It was touch and go for five years. Rose, with her trips and tantrums, so much younger than Sebastian. Finally, she ran away."

"But what happened?"

Belinda sighed. "Robin, dear, nobody knows. Of course, it was some man. We are sure of that much. For Sebastian found some letters. She must have walked down to the highway, somehow, and been picked up, and that was that. Sebastian *did* look for her. Detectives, you know. But he didn't want to hunt her like a criminal. And he so wanted to keep Annetta. Maybe he didn't try as hard as he could have. Anyway, poor Annetta— she can't forget her mother, nor forgive her. So that's why——"

My throat felt tight with sympathy. I knew what it was like to be abandoned, unloved. Now I could understand Annetta. I promised myself I would try to be her friend.

I finished my coffee and lay back. "Sometimes people do the most terrible things and they don't know," I said.

"I'm afraid that often they just don't care," Belinda told me.

I knew she was thinking about Rose.

"Perhaps that too," I agreed.

But I was thinking about myself, my reasons for coming to Cromwell Crossing with Jamie.

I closed my eyes. Belinda took the hint. She got to her feet. "I'll leave you, Robin. If I stay, I'll just go on and on, like always. Do you need an aspirin yet?"

I shook my head.

"Then nap." She patted the coverlet around my shoulders. "When you wake, you'll feel much better."

After she had gone, I tried to fall asleep. But, though my own fear seemed very far away now, my mind churned with the things Belinda had told me. Annetta's mother deserting her, and poor Jamie, always feeling as if he were responsible for his mother's death, always the outsider. His small bitter hints made sense now in a way that they never had before. It was no wonder Belinda had said the Cromwell family needed a change of luck.

Only Jamie and I knew that we were not the ones who could bring happiness to Cromwell Crossing. My heart ached for the big, gray-faced man in his castle on the mountain.

But later, after Ned had seen me, and Belinda had shown me proudly through the house, when Jamie and Annetta came back and drove me up the mountain, all my fear came flooding back again.

I shivered as Jamie helped me from the car. I dreaded going inside where I knew Sebastian and Michael would be waiting. I dreaded facing them, with the knowledge in my mind that someone had tried to kill me, wondering which one of them had done it, wondering why.

Annetta, always quick as a dancer on her feet, went

ahead, shouting, "We're back, Sebastian. Michael, we're back."

"Jamie," I said softly, "come upstairs with me. I have to talk to you, to show you the balustrade."

He grinned. "Okay. I might as well humor the invalid, I guess."

"Don't humor me," I retorted. "Just be willing to listen, and to use your eyes."

"Okay, I'll be willing," he answered.

But I knew he had made up his mind. He wouldn't be easy to convince. He had already decided not to believe me.

Chapter SIX

THE MAIN hall was empty. The portraits in their wide golden frames looked down at us, the men handsome, the women beautiful, all disapproving.

Jamie paused. "Now where's everybody gone to?"

"I want to go straight up," I said, relieved.

"Single-minded little thing, aren't you?" Jamie grinned.

"I have to be."

Suddenly sobered, he answered, "I hope you remember that, Robin."

Annetta yelled, "Bobby, Sebastian wants you."

I felt the familiar tingle of discomfort, but knowing why Annetta didn't like my name seemed to help a bit.

Jamie shrugged, led me to the open doors of Sebastian's wing. "We had better stop in."

I started to protest, then let it go. Another few minutes wouldn't matter.

Sebastian was stretched out on the big leather couch in his study. He raised his head. "Like any old man, I get to take a nap after lunch. You all right, girl?"

"It wasn't anything much," I told him, though even then I was beginning to feel a slow throb of pain spread from my shin down my leg.

"A nap might do you some good, too. Maria's going to bring you lunch on a tray."

"Where's Michael?" Annetta demanded.

"Looking the place over," Sebastian told her. "I expect you can track him down, if you try, and——" He chuckled. "I expect you will try."

Jamie and I left Sebastian, still teasing Annetta, and chuckling when she pouted.

We went up the wide spiral staircase slowly.

In our suite, with the door closed, Jamie said, "Okay, shoot. What's on your mind?"

I took some aspirin, then, wearily, I sat down on the sofa, hoping the pills would work quickly. "Jamie, somebody *did* try to kill me. I'm sure of it." That time my voice was steady, calm.

He gave me an impatient look. "Honestly, Robin, that was foolish enough when you were scared witless. But now——"

"It's true."

"Don't be ridiculous," he said angrily. "You're just trying to find a good excuse for backing out."

"No, Jamie. Someone had to shove, and shove hard, to get that heavy jardiniere off the balustrade. I saw the scrape marks, I tell you. Come out and see for yourself."

"All right, Robin. Show me."

I knew by his tone he was humoring me. I went ahead, through the bedroom. "You'll see," I was saying to Jamie, as we stepped out onto the balcony.

"See what?" It was Michael, leaning at the balustrade, his low voice as toneless as ever, but his lean face alive with mockery.

I stopped so suddenly that Jamie bumped into me.

Michael went on. "We did some small rearranging— I knew you'd as soon not be reminded of this morning."

I stared at the neat line of planters. There was no empty space now to show that one was missing. I moved closer. Dozens of scars marked the balustrade, scars where each of the planters had been moved.

I looked back at Michael. His light-gray eyes, curtained and shallow as before, watched me. For one wild moment, I wondered if I had imagined the whole thing, imagined even my own certainty. Then I heard that familiar ugly raw grating sound again, and jerked my head up. Further down the balcony, Henley was working at the balustrade.

He glanced at me, smiled a small tight smile, sunlight reflecting on his rimless glasses.

"All right now?" Henley asked.

I nodded, smiling back at him, suddenly reminded of that small gray bookkeeper at Greenley's and drawing a peculiar comfort from the memory.

"See what?" Michael asked again.

Jamie answered for me. "This little girl has an imagination just as large as she is small," he said in an indulgent voice. "She thinks somebody dumped the pot deliberately."

"Deliberately?" Michael's tall lean body straightened. His eyes met mine. "How odd. I wouldn't have suspected you were so fanciful, Robin."

Jamie said quickly, "She was just scared silly."

"Of course," Michael agreed, still watching me. "And I don't know you at all, do I, Robin? So, perhaps, you are always fanciful. Yet it is peculiar for you to turn a simple accident into an attempted murder. And that is what you're saying, isn't it?"

I couldn't answer him. I felt the strange force in him, and I knew what Belinda meant when she said he had the same, and even more, steel as Sebastian.

Michael went on. "Since you've only just come, why would anyone here want to hurt you?"

Again I couldn't reply. Time had caught again, stopped. I found myself clenching my fists as hard as I could, holding my breath, in a brief try for poise.

That time Michael meant to have an answer. He said, "Well?"

"I don't know," I said finally.

"Perhaps you have enemies—back there, where you came from—Los Angeles, did you say?" At my nod, he went on. "And they came here, sneaked in, and——"

"That's impossible," I told him.

A muscle twitched in his jaw. "Then, plainly, it doesn't make sense, does it?"

"I guess not," I whispered, knowing I was giving him the answer he wanted.

"And it would upset Sebastian terribly to think that——"

I said quickly, surprised, "But I don't intend to say anything to Sebastian. Why should I?"

I saw a faint flicker of relief cross Michael's tense face.

I added, "It wouldn't do any good."

"No." He looked at me as if we were alone, alone in an empty world. "No, it wouldn't do any good, Robin."

I was suddenly frightened again. The warm sun seemed to have cooled. A covey of clouds spread moving shadows across the balcony.

I was certain that Michael not only believed me, but was sure that I was right. He had moved the planters so that the single scar would blend into the many fresh ones.

He had hoped to convince me that I had imagined the attempt on my life. And I knew, somehow I knew, he had given up that hope. But, just the same, he was satisfied. And I understood that. He was protecting Sebastian. "Responsible Michael," Belinda had said. Yes, I could already see that for myself. Then Jamie and I were on one side, and Michael on the other.

He turned to Jamie then. "If your wife really is afraid, perhaps you should plan on leaving."

I wondered if I only imagined the faint stress on the word *wife*.

But Jamie hooted. "Fat chance! We came here to be with Sebastian, and we'll be here quite awhile."

A faint glimmer of amusement appeared in Michael's bottomless eyes, but no smile touched his straight lips. He said dryly, "I thought as much, Jamie."

"Making a mountain out of a molehill," Jamie grumbled. "Robin, honey, you know what? You surprise me."

"I guess I've been an awful fool." I tried to make my voice rueful. "It all happened so suddenly, and I couldn't think how a thing that big——"

The amusement in Michael's eyes was deep and plain. He understood that my backing down was no more than a pretense. He said soothingly, "But accidents *do* happen." And added surprisingly, "So perhaps you should be careful."

That was either a threat, or a warning. I didn't know which. I didn't try to think it out. I said lightly, "Oh, there won't be any more accidents, I'm sure."

"Does your leg bother you much?" he asked.

"Just a little. But I think I'll go in and lie down."

"That's a good idea," Michael told me, turning away, to join Henley further down the balcony.

It was then, watching him, that I noticed the limp for the first time. He was taller even than Sebastian, very straight, with wide rigid shoulders, and a long solid stride that almost hid the stiffness in his left leg. The sun made his dark short-cropped hair glint blue-black. He bent to help Henley, and I could see the muscles move under his white shirt.

I went inside, just as glad as I knew he must be that we had found an excuse to end the uncomfortable conversation.

"It's a good thing you came to your senses," Jamie said. I didn't answer him. Maria had tapped at the door, came in at my call, bringing us a tray.

"All right now?" she nodded, smiling hopefully.

"I'm fine," I told her, though my leg still throbbed, but less painfully now.

Maria went out, still nodding, her round dusky face pleased.

Jamie ate his sandwiches, while I, not hungry, lay down on my bed.

Soon he went out on the balcony again, and I heard him talking with Michael. Their voices made a wordless rumbling counterpoint to my circling thoughts.

I told myself that I was redheaded and green-eyed and quite capable of taking care of myself. I fought down my terror until it was a small throbbing pain, a weak quivering, no more than the drugged pain in my cut and stitched leg.

I reminded myself of all the nothing I *had* ever had, and all the nothing I *would* ever have if I faltered now.

That chance meeting with Jamie outside the Commodore Hotel had given me an opportunity, and if I turned away from it, I would never have another.

I dared not turn away. I dared not be driven away. Jamie was right. You had to fight for what you wanted, take chances, tangle with risk.

I drowsed, bright images drifting before my closed eyes. A little while, just a little while in Cromwell Crossing, and then. . . .

Later, Jamie came in, his sandy hair tousled. "Well?"

"Well what, Jamie?"

"Do we pack and run because you've got cold feet? Or do we stay and go on as planned?"

"We stay, Jamie." I smiled at him. "I may be fanciful, as Michael says, but I'm not so fainthearted as all that."

Jamie looked surprised, then grinned. "Convinced, are you?"

I didn't answer him.

He went on. "That's one of Michael's special talents. He's a great convincer."

"Is he?"

"You had me worried for a while." Jamie flung himself down on the chaise. "I saw our whole plan go up in smoke."

I managed to smile. "Or down in a planter."

"Forget it, Robin."

"How long will Michael be staying?" I asked.

"We didn't talk about it," Jamie said.

"Do you think he's suspicious?"

"About what?"

"You and me, Jamie. About why we're here. That maybe we aren't married."

"I don't think so. But you can't tell much about Michael."

"I know." But, somehow, I knew he was suspicious. I knew he was on the other side of that line, facing Jamie and me; he must be convinced, just as Sebastian must be convinced.

Jamie got up, stuck his hands in his pockets, took a few restless steps. "I hope it doesn't take too long. I already begin to feel hemmed in."

"So do I," I agreed fervently.

"But so far so good, Robin. And afterwards——"

I turned my head away. "Afterwards——" I whispered, a ripple of fear twisting through me. "If there is an afterwards——"

But Jamie didn't answer me.

We had just finished having dinner together.

Sebastian sat back in his chair, toying with his unlit pipe, looking at us, at each of us, in turn.

"All together again," he said finally, in a voice husky with satisfaction. "I tell you, I began to think I'd never manage to live to see the time."

He smiled at me, his dark-blue eyes full of surprising youth, and I could see the man behind the gaunt gray lines of his rugged face. The bawdy, lusty, life-loving man he was.

I found myself thinking about the redheaded sailor my mother had once told me about, told me about on a rare visit, in a rare burst of confidence or defensiveness. A laughing, redheaded sailor. I wondered if he would have aged to be like Sebastian.

Sebastian went on, "And you, Robin—you—that's another name for hope, in my book."

I felt the answering smile on my lips begin to freeze in the dry ice of guilt. I swallowed hard.

But Jamie laughed. "Sebastian, if you're talking about what I believe you're talking about, you sure do let your mind run ahead, don't you?" Meanwhile, he gave me a sly teasing wink.

I looked away from him, annoyed that he seemed to take so much joy in the deception Sebastian so plainly didn't suspect. It was one thing to do it; it was another to pretend it was a game.

Michael was staring at me, his lean face as expressionless as ever, his dark brows straight over the deep-set pale eyes.

I folded my napkin carefully, concentrating on the smooth edges of the heavy linen.

Sebastian said, "At my stage of the game, a man's lucky if he has something to hope for. So don't grudge me." He added in his slow, breath-saving way, "And something good to look back on as well."

"Oh, no," Annetta groaned. "Sebastian, darling, please —no family stuff. Michael's home, and Jamie's home— and couldn't we——"

Michael cut in. "We can and we shall, but later, Annetta."

She gave him a pout, but when he looked at her, as expressionless as always, she turned it into her brilliant warm smile.

I wondered what good things Sebastian had to look back on, thinking of all the sadness there must have been in his life.

He nodded at me. "Annetta's right. I was going to talk about the family. Did you get to see the old house? It was built to last, you know. Made to withstand Comanches, and weather, and time itself. Even my forefathers were dynasty-minded. Like me."

"It's a lovely place," I told him.

"Its meaning is more lovely than its appearance. There's got to be something that's more than physical. It's the family, the generations going on."

Michael suddenly pushed back his chair and stood up. He leaned at the table for a moment, his shoulders rigid under his tan jacket. Finally, he said, "Brandy, Sebastian?" At his father's quick nod, Michael limped from the room.

Sebastian waited until the door was closed, then mumbled, "I guess I could have talked a long time without starting in on that right in front of him. Poor boy—he's got a memory as long as I have." Sebastian sighed and pushed himself up. "You have your brandy in the big room; then come into the study." He smiled at me, a small tilt at the corners of his faintly blue lips. "I have a

little something for you, Robin. A small surprise to say
I'm mighty pleased. You can call it a wedding present,
if you want to. But I'll just call it a 'knowing-you' present."

"But you don't have to," I protested. "I mean—really
Sebastian—being here is——"

"Being here. Stuck in the middle of nowhere. Why,
Robin, being here's nothing to you. Not yet. Maybe sometime it will. Maybe someday you'll get to love the high
country. But for now, it's just having you with us, part of
us, that counts."

He went out, walking slowly, a tall gaunt tired man.
Annetta followed him, demanding, "What is it? Come
on, Sebastian, whisper to me. What do you have? Where
did you get it? I won't tell. Sebastian, please——"

Jamie grinned, silently held up his hand, his forefinger
and thumb making an A-okay sign at me.

"Jamie——"

"In like Flynn." He laughed. "You ought to be sending
out sparkles instead of looking as if you've lost your best
friend."

"I feel ashamed," I whispered.

"I feel ashamed," he mocked me. "So, when the time
comes you can apologize sweetly before you cry all the
way to the bank." He got up. "I'll go direct Michael to
the living room."

I too rose and said, "I don't want any brandy. I'll go
up, and you can call me when——"

"Running away to hide!" Jamie made a sound of dis-
gust. "I can't figure you out. I don't even want to. Keep
your mind on what you're supposed to be doing."

"All right. Brandy and the living room it is."

"That's better." He gave me a sudden boyish grin.
"You're making me work harder at keeping you in line
than at working on Sebastian."

"We've hardly been here a day," I told him.

His face became sullen. "Listen, Robin, honey, it seems like all of ten years to me."

It seemed to me, too, as if months had passed since the night before when I'd felt those melancholy waves reach out at me from the shadowed house.

But I said, "Jamie, why don't you forget the past? It doesn't matter any more. You're all grown now."

"What?"

"Belinda told me."

"Told you what, Robin, honey?"

"About your mother dying. And what it meant to you, being left alone, not having her. But you're old enough, Jamie, to realize, to understand—you don't have to——"

"Two-bit psychiatry," he cut in, his whisper deep, hard. "You think I brought you here to remake me, or to read me a sermon, Robin, honey? You're playing a con game, so play it straight."

"I deserve that," I said softly.

He didn't answer. He shrugged, and went into the hall. I heard him speak to Michael.

A soft, strangely accented voice saying my name made me jump. Maria stood in the kitchen doorway.

"Robin? Robin, your leg is all better now?"

"It doesn't hurt. Just a twinge once in a while."

"Good," she said, her sober eyes pleased. "Now you will forget it."

"Until the stitches have to come out."

"If there is anything—" She faltered, her plump hands made a gesture. "I will help you, Robin."

"Thank you, Maria."

"Anything, Robin."

Her black eyes held mine, sending me a message I couldn't read, but a message that I knew was there.

I found myself whispering another thanks as Jamie called from the door.

We had our brandy. The fragile glasses were sparkling crystal. The huge room, though aglow with pink light from the chandeliers, seemed full of shadows.

I sipped my drink, watching as Michael, silently, refilled his glass and Jamie's once, and then again.

Jamie spoke of San Francisco with too much eagerness, too much longing. I knew Michael could hear it, for his lean face seemed to tighten, and his pale eyes became even more shallow.

I was relieved when Annetta came dashing in, to cry, "Come on. Sebastian says bring the bottle and get ready. He's all set."

"Bring the bottle!" Jamie laughed. "You hear that, Michael? This is big, it is."

Michael didn't answer.

Chapter SEVEN

I PAUSED in the main hall, Michael and Jamie with me.

The portraits seemed to stare at me crying "Impostor" from their wide golden frames.

"Family?" I asked.

Sebastian, a mischievous smile on his face, answered me from the doorway of the study. "Some of them are. Some not." He chuckled. "My father, that's him at the and his wife. And, then, from his description, his father needed family portraits, so he had them painted. Him and his wife. And, then, from his description, his father and mother. They're at the end. And when the four of them didn't seem enough to him, he had a few more done, just to fill up the walls, I guess."

"And you?"

"I'm down there, too." Sebastian chuckled again. "I don't get left out of anything around here. And Michael's mother, too, of course."

I felt Jamie's sudden movement. I took his hand, felt his fingers curl around mine.

Drawing Jamie to me, I walked slowly down the hall, looking at each of the paintings in turn. The first Michael Cromwell, as seen by the artist through the eyes of Sebastian's father, was an imposing man. His pale-blue eyes stared at me challengingly. His black mustache drooped to his chin. If, instead of a big Western hat, he'd worn a bandanna around his dark hair and a gold hoop in one ear, he would have been a perfect stand-in for a pirate off the Spanish Main. His wife, in brocade, had a wistful expression, but a firm jaw. Sebastian's father himself had a craggy face, dark-blue eyes, and long dark sideburns. His mother had been fair and beautiful with the same faint smile as Sebastian.

I didn't have time to look at the others. Sebastian said, "Come along now, before I burst, and Annetta, too. One of these days we'll see you get done, and you'll hang up there, beside the rest of them. When the time comes, you can drag down the phonies and fill them up with real Cromwells."

My cheeks were burning as we all went into the study. I felt as if the portraits had sneered at me.

Sebastian sat down behind the huge desk. He leaned back. "Robin, you're going to have to choose." His dark-blue eyes moved over to me in that quick young look. "But you just take your time. Don't worry about it. Just decide for yourself." He went on, "Now you come here, and have a look."

I went to the desk. But what I saw, suddenly, for the

first time, was a gun. I stared at it, then raised my eyes to Sebastian's face.

He chuckled. "No, girl, not that. But, if you're going to live in the high country, you had better get used to seeing a gun or two, and get over staring at them as if they were snakes."

"I never saw one before in my life," I said.

"Never? Well, you have now. And there isn't a house out here where you wouldn't find a handgun like this, and more, scattered around, and some rifles put handy, too." Sebastian shoved the gun aside. "But since you don't know them, figure on not touching them. They're all loaded, you know. Not for play, but for serious business."

"We'll teach you," Annetta cried. "Jamie and me! We can go target-shooting together like we used to."

"Oh, I don't know," I said, laughing a little. "I don't think I want very much to know about guns."

"But it's fun," she insisted.

Sebastian cut in, "Now, Robin, here, look. You'll see what I meant about choosing." He took a small sack from the pocket of his frontier shirt. There was a faint earthy odor in the air. I noticed it and forgot it as Sebastian's gnarled hands worked unsteadily at a drawstring, then yanked it open, and upended the sack over the desk.

Bits of glitter, sparkles, rainbow facets flashed and danced against the dark wood.

Henley, hovering at Sebastian's shoulder, gave a soft half sigh. Annetta giggled. Michael, in the easy chair, stretched out his long legs.

My eyes moved back to the desk. I looked at what I thought were chips of beautiful glass, at irregular polished stones. I wondered why Sebastian was offering them to me.

"Go on, girl," he said. "Take yourself a good look,

and then take your pick of one, or two. Depending on what you want to do."

Bewildered, I glanced at Jamie. His face was avid, twisted with greed.

Annetta chortled, "She doesn't know, Sebastian. She doesn't recognize diamonds when she sees them."

"Diamonds?" I gasped.

"Diamonds, rubies, a couple of small emeralds." Sebastian laughed. "Go on. Handle them. They don't bite or burn. Pick some. My knowing-you gift, girl."

My fingers curled in the blue silk of my dress. I backed away from the desk. "Oh, I couldn't, Sebastian. I just couldn't. They're so valuable, must be worth a fortune—I'd never——"

"That's my wife," Jamie said suddenly. "She'll turn down a diamond every time."

I shook my head. "But don't you see——"

Michael moved abruptly. I looked toward him and caught a brief expression of bewilderment on his face before he quickly masked it.

I knew then. I was sure. He *was* suspicious of Jamie and me. He was watching. I made up my mind that I had to be careful. If Michael guessed, he would spoil everything. Jamie and I would have to leave Cromwell Crossing empty-handed. All my bright dreams would be finished for good. I would go back to nothing again.

I looked at Sebastian.

"I always get my way," he was telling me. "Don't you already know that, girl? Now, either you pick your present from out of this mess of stones, or I pick it for you."

I knew that Michael was waiting. I could feel waves of fury flowing at me from Jamie. Yet I didn't want Sebastian to give me so valuable a gift. I liked him too much to accept a present which was a symbol, to me, of his love and expectations.

"But, Sebastian——" I mumbled.

He cut in gently. "Don't you know, girl? Don't you understand what your coming here means to me? What it means having Jamie and his wife home and safe and the Cromwell name to go on and on?"

I clenched my fists at my sides.

I didn't know what I was going to answer.

Annetta saved me. She cried, "Didn't you see the two stones I was wearing last night, Robin?"

I noticed gratefully that Belinda's admonition had been successful. Annetta had begun to call me by my first name. It made me feel more like myself.

"Two diamonds," she went on. "Made into earrings. I had them on when you came." She tossed her dark hair so that the curls danced. "Sebastian gave them to me last year for my birthday."

I kept my eyes on the desk. The bright stones winked at me like sparkling teardrops.

Jamie chuckled, breaking the short silence. "Now when and how did you get your hands on that haul, Sebastian?"

Sebastian grinned.

Jamie went on. "I hope you've built yourself a good strong safe. That's not a bundle you can leave around loose for anybody to get hold of."

Sebastian gave him a mischievous smile. "Don't you worry about that, boy. I've got me a good safe. A fine one."

Michael, sounding amused, said suddenly, "Robin, you're having a terrible time making up your mind. Maybe you had better just close your eyes and take a handful?"

"Yes, Robin. Just close your eyes and grab," Annetta chanted. "Just grab a handful."

"Sebastian, why don't we wait—let me think about it?" I said finally.

The old man's laugh boomed out, sounding hardy and healthy. "You're making too much out of it, girl. These stones here, that's part of the Cromwell spirit I was telling you about last night. Remember that Galveston hurricane and tidal wave in 1957 or so? That was a fine mess. All that looting—bad people moving in to scavenge—and to salvage, of course." He shook his head, grinned. "This was fine salvage, too." He looked up at Henley, "Eh, Henley? Fine salvage?"

"So that's where you got them," Jamie breathed.

Henley's rimless glasses twinkled, hiding his eyes as he nodded. "A good job, Sebastian."

"More yours than mine," Sebastian told him. And then to me, "It sure was a good job, girl. I got these at a fine price. No price hardly, when you come to think of it, and not a one of them traceable either."

"You mean they're stolen?" I gasped.

"In a way, yes, and in a way, no." Sebastian hunched over the stones. "Since I've scared you half to death with my storytelling, I'll do the work then." His big gnarled hand hovered, fingers touching and withdrawing, then picked up two green stones. "Emeralds, then. Emeralds for an emerald-eyed girl." He held out his palm. "Go on, Robin. They'll make you a fine pair of earrings one of these days."

"Like mine," Annetta said softly. "Just like mine, Robin, but not diamonds."

I let Sebastian put the shining bits into my hand, and curl my fingers around them. "Thank you, Sebastian," I whispered, feeling as if he were handing me, along with the stones, his heart and his trust. And then, before I could stop myself, I said, "But I really don't deserve such a gift."

The room was suddenly too quiet.

I wanted to bite my wayward tongue for having blurted out the words that had been echoing in my mind.

But Sebastian laughed. "Who does deserve it, girl? Maybe not you. But surely not me."

I closed the door of the suite, and leaned against it wearily. I felt as if I had done a long hard day's work. My shin throbbed. Every bone in my body ached from long endured tension. The emeralds seemed to burn the flesh of my still clenched fingers.

"That is the first bonus for you," Jamie said. "And what a bonus! Now do you see why all this is worth your while, and mine?"

I didn't answer him. I went through the sitting room into my bedroom. The stones made a small sharp whisper as I dropped them on the mahogany dresser.

Jamie, following, went on jubilantly, "I thought for a minute I was going to have to slug you. And then I figured for sure you'd blown the whole thing sky-high. 'I really don't deserve such a gift,'" he mocked me, repeating my words in a whining falsetto. "But you've got him. You can say anything to Sebastian and he hears what he wants to."

"You can have the emeralds, Jamie."

"Your first bonus?" Jamie grinned. "You're awfully generous. Don't say that twice. I might take you up on it. They'll bring a good price one of these days." He went on, "You ought to be on the stage. Your talents are wasted. Robin, your face when you realized what he dumped out on that desk! And then, when you were protesting you didn't——"

"It wasn't an act, Jamie."

"Wasn't it?" He chuckled. "No, I guess not. I was surprised myself. I never knew about that particular haul. The old devil—he can be sharp when he wants to. So you had better be careful, Robin."

"Careful?" I repeated.

"Don't let him fool you. He's got his eyes open."

"I hope he does," I said bitterly. "I hope he realizes the truth, and throws us both out."

Jamie's pale eyes narrowed. He grabbed me by the shoulders. "You had better not hope for that," he said through his teeth. "We'll both end up with nothing."

"Maybe that's what I want."

"You want—you want——" He shook me so hard that my head rocked back and forth. "It's too late for that, Robin, honey. If you wreck it now, I'm wrecked for good. For good and all. Do you understand me?" He dropped his hands away, patted my cheek. But his voice was low, thin, no longer boyish. "We're going to go through with it as planned, and you're going to back me up all the way. No fake scare, and no fake conscience, is going to tie me to this place forever. Get it?"

"I didn't say I was giving it up, Jamie." I moved away from him, taking slow cautious steps.

But Jamie was grinning again. "There's my girl. I didn't really believe you were ready to beat a hasty retreat."

"But I can't help feeling ashamed," I said.

"I don't care how you feel. Just what you do." He patted my cheek again. "You wait, just wait until you have all that bread, all those fine bills, in your hot little hands. Then you can be ashamed, and it won't cost you a thing, either." He got a pillow and spread. "I guess it's time to turn in. Good night, Robin, honey. Sleep tight."

"I'll dream about all those bills," I said.

His smile broadened, but his wide-spaced eyes were still on my face. "You do that," he said easily, and then went into the sitting room, closing the door between us.

Jamie's suddenly relaxed manner didn't make me forget the glimpse of that totally deep uncaring ruthlessness I had seen in him momentarily—his pale-blue eyes narrowed, his mouth grim, his voice threatening.

Once again, I wondered which one was the real Jamie.

I shivered as I readied myself for bed.

Chapter *EIGHT*

THE MORNING sun laid a yellow haze over the valley, and rimmed the terrace with a golden path. The blue of the sky stretched endlessly to a blurred horizon where a few billowy clouds hung motionless in the thin air.

I leaned my elbows on the balustrade, studying the strange blend of colors and shapes below. The wind eroded towering rock that gleamed with reds in every imaginable shade; the grays and greens and blues of angular cedar and spruce; the faint purple and mustard yellow of spiny sage.

It was hard to believe that only the morning before I had seen a dark swooping shadow cut the sunlight above me, hard to believe that there was danger where beauty crowded beauty until it nearly hurt my eyes to look at it.

I glanced down at the small white tape that tingled on my shin. Yes. The black shadow *had* swooped at me. The jagged stone shard *had* gouged a bloody path in my flesh.

I had been lying in the shade, dreaming, pretending to myself that I had come home at last, had found the place where I belonged. Those foolish dreams were gone now. Yet I knew the mountains had taken a strange possession of me. The mountains, the valley below. Even the house itself.

Those foolish dreams were gone, but, once again in sunlight, I could hardly remember the air of melancholy, that quality of menace, which had so touched me the day before.

I found myself looking at the valley, smiling, as if I had actually come to Cromwell Crossing as Jamie's true bride—come, loved and cherished, to the family I had always longed for.

Then, as a car door slammed, the spell was broken. A distant voice, Annetta's, cried, "Let's go then, Jamie."

Behind me, the house was silent, a vast crouching pile of old gray rock with tiered balconies and glinting windows.

A motor whirred and caught. There was a shattering of gravel as wheels spun in a fast turn. I leaned over the balustrade to look, and saw a glint of metal moving in the shadow of the trees. I knew that Annetta and Jamie were going into town.

I looked at the house again. It seemed to hold its breath, waiting. But what was it waiting for? I asked myself.

I went inside. I stopped to powder my nose, to paint my mouth a defiant pink, and to brush my coppery hair. I had dressed carefully, high heels and nylons, and a pink skirt and pink-and-white blouse as armor against whatever the day might bring. My green eyes peered back at me from the mirror with a scared child's open stare.

"Stop it," I said aloud, and then, hearing the quaver, repeated, "Stop it!" this time with firmness. But my eyes dropped away from their own frightened scrutiny.

The emeralds were still on the dresser where I had

dropped them the night before. I wrapped them into a handkerchief and knotted it tightly. Then I dropped it into a drawer.

I took a long slow breath and went into the sitting room. At least, I had successfully avoided seeing Jamie, which was what I'd wanted. But I knew that was foolish of me. What I really wanted was to avoid my own conscience, and no amount of hiding in my suite would accomplish that, nor would lingering on the balcony and allowing my head to fill with silly dreams dispel my sense of guilt.

I gave an impatient shrug, and reminded myself that I hadn't yet had morning coffee. Maria, possibly Henley, would be in the copper- and plant-filled kitchen.

I went into the empty hall to the oval landing and hurried down the steep staircase. With the pink chandeliers switched off, the main floor was dim. Echoes of old sad memories drifted in the shadowed corners.

The portraits stared down at me, and I returned their interest, staring back as I moved from one to the other. Sebastian, looking younger, but mischievous as now. And Michael's mother—Jamie's mother, too, I reminded myself, remembering how his fingers had curled around my hand when Sebastian identified the portrait the night before. And it was Jamie who resembled her. She had the same light-blue eyes, the sandy curls. Next to her, more recently done to judge by her strapless evening gown, was a young woman—tall, dark-haired. I remembered Belinda's description of Ayren. This must be she, I thought. Ayren, before she died. She returned my inspection gravely, imperiously.

I found myself backing away from Ayren's portrait. If she, so self-possessed, so sure of herself, had been no match for Cromwell Crossing, then how dare I attempt to storm it?

The old house still held its breath, waited.

I found myself running, silent footsteps on the thick rugs. I was breathing hard when I thrust open the door of the kitchen, like a medieval criminal racing for sanctuary.

The room was full of sunlight. Maria and Henley were sitting with Michael. They had been laughing together, but the sound of it faded as I came in.

Michael turned, a smile still on his lips. It changed his whole face, brought a depth and shine to his light-gray eyes, softened the hard angle of his jaw, gave warmth to a face which had the chill of stone.

It was the first time, I knew suddenly, that I had actually seen him smile. I realized that the armor I had put on thinking it would help me face the day and my own conscience had been actually chosen as protection against him.

"Good morning, Robin," Michael said gravely. "Sit down."

His smile was gone now, though I still sensed its warmth as I greeted him, then Maria and Henley. The two of them bustled around me. Michael sat back, watching.

After I had coffee and the waffle Maria insisted on, Michael said, "Jamie went into town with Annetta."

"I thought I heard them leave."

"You're an early riser for a city girl, aren't you?" Then, "You *are* a city girl, of course?"

"I suppose so. At least I call Los Angeles home."

I looked around uncomfortably. Henley had left on such silent feet that I hadn't until that moment realized that he was gone. And Maria, saying, "More coffee on the stove," went out through the back door.

I was alone with Michael. I warned myself to be careful. If he guessed why I was here with Jamie. . . .

"Want more coffee?" he was asking.

I shook my head.

"Cigarette?"

I accepted one, thinking of it as more armor. But I had rarely smoked and didn't like it, so the first puff made me choke and cough, and I could feel my face purple with the effort I made to keep from exploding.

Michael had leaned across the table to light my cigarette, then without straightening, he had lit his own. Now he shook his head, suddenly grinned. "Put that out; you're no smoker."

I answered him by taking a small careful drag. "It just went down the wrong way," I said at last.

"I see." The grin faded. He asked suddenly, "How did you happen to meet Jamie?"

I told him just about what I had told Sebastian before, again sticking as close to the truth as I reasonably could.

Michael listened without comment until I had finished. Then, leaning toward me again, he said, "You knew him for a month? Just a month, Robin?"

"And I was sure——" I told him. "I knew——"

"A month. Rather hasty for a decision like that. For marriage."

"But when you know——"

"And did you? Do you? Can you say that you really know Jamie?"

I stared at Michael, thinking, knowing that he was waiting for an answer, but unable to give him one.

Did I know Jamie? No. No, of course not. I had seen his boyish open grin, heard his quick rebellious words, sensed a deep core of bitterness in him. I had watched him change from sweetness to cruelty, and back to sweetness again. Jamie was like a broken mirror, each reflection a slightly distorted image.

No, I didn't know Jamie. I couldn't figure him out.

Later, I understood. Jamie looked like a perfect human being, but he had been born with some small element missing—been born, or perhaps grown, without that small invisible element that some men call "love," others call "soul," still others call "empathy." He existed in and for himself, and in and for what he alone wanted. He became son, lover, friend, brother, even husband, as each role was expected of him. But each character remained an isolated role which he played without any relevance except to his own needs. He was a machine man, a nicely constructed computer, keyed just to his own desires.

Michael had asked me, "Can you say that you really know Jamie?"

I busied myself tamping out my half-finished cigarette, getting the coffeepot and refilling Michael's cup and mine. Seated again, I asked, "Does anyone ever know another person?"

"That hardly answers my question, Robin."

"All right, then. I think I do know Jamie."

"Then you must see that Cromwell Crossing isn't good for him. He shouldn't have come home."

"But why?" I protested. "It *is* his home, Mic___."

Michael's dark brows angled over his ___s. "That doesn't mean it's good for him."

I wondered just what Michael was leading up to. I said, "He wanted me to meet his father, his family, Michael. To——"

"No, Robin. No, he didn't. That's not what he was after." Michael's voice, toneless, paused, then went on, "Well, maybe that, too, but——"

I waited.

"And I think it would be best if you both ft. Right away, Robin."

"But I don't understand."

"Don't you?"

Of course, I understood. Michael had already seen through Jamie's scheme, guessed the truth, and was warning me that it wouldn't work—because he wouldn't let it work.

Again, I waited.

"It isn't personal, Robin. I hope you know that."

"It's very personal when someone tries to kill me," I retorted.

He grinned, a quick white flash of teeth in his tanned face, a flash that instantly died. "I wondered when some of that redheaded temper was going to show up." Then, "We had decided it was an accident, hadn't we?"

"We had decided to pretend it was, Michael." I went on. "And you haven't answered me anyway."

"No," he said soberly.

"You're just telling me to pack up Jamie and drag him out of here."

"That's right," Michael agreed.

I drew a long slow breath, thinking as quickly as I could. I decided that some degree of candor was best. "I'm willing to leave, more than willing, Michael. But Jamie feels that he should have a settlement. He wants to be on his own. Now that——"

I had intended to say, "Now that we're married, he feels Sebastian owes him his independence," but I couldn't make myself say those words.

Michael said slowly, "So that's why he came home?"

I nodded. "And that isn't so wrong, is it, Michael? Jamie does have the right to——"

Michael cut in. "What about you?"

"Me?"

His pale eyes met my glance full on. "You and the settlement?"

"I told you I was willing to leave."

"But without it, Robin?"

"That's up to Jamie." I took a long careful breath again. "But I won't be driven away, Michael."

He pushed back his chair, got up, left me without another word.

I stared at the door as it closed gently behind him. Then I reached for my coffee cup. My hand shook. I made a tight fist and held it as hard as I could. Then I relaxed my fingers. In a moment, blessing my friend at Greenley's, I felt more at ease. I finished my coffee and went upstairs to the balcony again.

I struggled and heaved and shoved until I had gotten the green chaise out of doors. I settled down, my hands linked behind my head, studying a ring of cottony clouds that had drifted closer, and going over in my mind the conversation I had just had with Michael. My cards were on the table now. All but one. I hoped that my honesty with Michael would help. Perhaps he could persuade Sebastian to give Jamie his way. I wondered if Michael could do that, if he would even try.

A shadow fell over me. I knew, instinctively, before I even looked up, straightened, that it was Michael again.

"Skydreaming?" he asked.

"Just thinking."

"Oh?" He leaned against the balustrade. "Who brought the chaise out for you?"

"I did."

"That's pretty big for you to handle, Robin. You could have asked me. I would have been glad to."

I glanced at him, then looked away, toward the valley. "I'm used to doing things for myself, Michael."

I warned myself to be wary. I had told him why Jamie and I had come to Cromwell Crossing. Now I must be sure not to give him a weapon to use against us.

"Since we've stopped pretending that falling planter was an accident, Michael, can you tell me why it happened? Who was responsible?"

He didn't answer me.

"But you know," I said angrily.

He still didn't answer.

"Was it you?" I demanded.

"Robin——" he began harshly; then he stopped for a moment. He went on more gently, "You know I was in the car with Jamie. We had just pulled in."

"An odd coincidence," I told him, smiling just a little. "We both know such things do happen."

"Then someone else. Someone in the house——"

"I've told you that you and Jamie should leave. What else is there to say?"

"You haven't given me a reason."

"You know the reason." His face had closed, gone expressionless. His light eyes were curtained. "You feel it in your bones," he went on softly.

Yes. I knew the reason. I could picture again the black swooping shadow, and hear the rolling echoes of the explosive crash of the large jardiniere on the terrace. I huddled more deeply into the chaise and, when I moved, a slow throb of pain moved into my knee from the cut below. Yes. I knew the reason. In my mind and in my bones.

For safety's sake, for my life's sake, I ought to pack now, to go; if necessary, to leave Jamie here alone. But there were reasons why I should stay, compelling reasons, bright images from the life I might have if I stayed.

Michael had turned away, so that all I could see was his unsmiling profile and the line of his wide shoulders. His fists, resting on the balustrade, were white-knuckled with tension.

He said tonelessly, "Sebastian has decided, you know. Nothing is going to change his mind. Not unless Jamie goes to work, and even then——"

"Then Jamie's his father's son."

Michael looked around at me. "We won't argue that."

With a shrug that said plainly he had finished with the subject, Michael offered to show me around the house. I hesitated, not sure I wanted to go with him. The line between us was clearly drawn. The less time I spent with him, the better it would be.

He seemed to know what was in my mind.

"Then get Jamie to give you the grand tour," he said, turning away abruptly.

I watched him limp along the length of the balcony. Now, perversely, I wished I had gone with him. A bird trilled a high sweet song from a spruce below. Suddenly, I felt unbearably alone.

I pushed myself out of the chaise. I started to shove it inside, but left it when I heard a knock at the door.

It was Henley to tell me that Sebastian would like to see me if I wasn't busy. As I went to the stairs, I glanced through the open door across the hall. Michael was sitting at a paper-scattered desk. He was speaking in a low toneless voice on the telephone. He glanced up at me, then deliberately looked away.

I wondered how he had gotten to his room without using any of the windows that fronted on the balcony, and decided that I must be sure to get Jamie to show me around the house. The more I knew about it, the better off I would be.

With Henley walking softly behind me, I went down to Sebastian's study. The old man was stretched out on the black leather sofa. His string tie hung loose at his throat, his shirt collar was unbuttoned. A slow grin tipped the corner of his lips.

"Left you all alone, did they?" Sebastian asked.

"Jamie and Annetta? I guess they thought I was still asleep."

"But you weren't. That's good. Then, if you don't object, sit down and keep an old man company."

"Old?" I teased.

"Yes, that's me. An old man—though I admit, when I

look at you, girl, there's entire periods when I forget it."

"Some day or other in your life, you kissed the blarney stone." I laughed.

"Never did. And always," his dark-blue eyes twinkled at me, "at least, almost always, I tell the straight truth."

He was quiet for a few minutes then, and when he spoke, it was to ask, "Do you like to read aloud, by any chance?"

"I've never tried," I told him, adding silently, "I never had anybody to read aloud to."

"Henley, there—" Sebastian turned his head to grin at the small gray man near the desk "—he tries and he doesn't much like it, and I admit, neither do I. But I like to listen."

"Do you want to see if you like to listen to me read, Sebastian?"

"I was going to suggest it. Henley, where's the book?"

I took the book Henley offered me, a thick one, with well-worn covers and thumbed pages.

"It's a history of this state," Sebastian told me. "You might as well learn a little about your new home while you're at it."

The book suddenly felt heavy in my hands. But I asked, "Where did you leave off, Sebastian?"

"Oh, I've been through it before, maybe a hundred times. Now, let's see. You start—well, maybe when General Kearney came in. Back when we made ourselves a territory. About twenty years before my folks moved in, and we've been here, and around, ever since. Even before Billy the Kid made a big name for himself unloading lead in Lincoln County down south. Maybe that's why it means so much to me. The high country, and the family, all mixed up together. Means *too* much to me, maybe."

I found the place and started to read; I soon realized that Jamie's father knew the text so well he was able to mumble it along with me.

Soon Sebastian stopped me. "You've got a good clear voice. Not like Henley here. He mumbles and grumbles it out like a wheezing elevator. But that's because he's a scrub-farm Texan, and our history kind of hurts him."

Henley's glasses twinkled, but he didn't answer.

"And, girl, while you're stopped," Sebastian said, "maybe you'd reach me my pipe. It ought to be there on the desk."

I looked, but the pipe wasn't there. I glanced up at the mantel. The pipe lay tipped against Sebastian's gun. I eyed the pipe, then picked it up cautiously, not wanting to allow my fingers even to brush the lethal steel-blue barrel.

Sebastian chuckled. "See that, Henley?" And to me, "Don't worry, girl. The safety's on. She won't go off like a firecracker."

I smiled at his teasing and handed him the pipe. His big veined hand closed around it.

"Ah, that's good. Not that I smoke it any more. But I do like to squeeze it every little bit." Then, "Go on, Robin. Read some more if you don't object."

I cleared my suddenly tight throat. I found myself thinking about the redheaded sailor who had bequeathed to me my hair color, but not a name. I wondered if, because of him, I had always looked for the father I'd never had; if, because of him, I was drawn irresistibly to Sebastian. I gave myself a hard mental shake and sneered cynically in Jamie's words: "Two-bit psychiatry." I told myself that what I felt didn't matter. It was urgent only that Sebastian like me.

I began to read again. Sebastian kept up with me for a little while, then his mumbling was stilled.

Henley touched my shoulder. I looked at Sebastian. He was sleeping, bluish lips silently moving, reiterating the words of the history which meant so much to him.

Chapter *NINE*

I WENT back to the kitchen.

"Is there something?" Maria asked. "Shall I serve you lunch in the dining room?"

I looked at the sunshine on the indoor garden she had planted under the windows and the soft glow of the pots on the wall.

"Could I eat here?" I asked. "With you?"

Her dusky face brightened with a wide smile. "Wherever you want, Robin. Whatever you want."

I seated myself at the round table, hands folded in my lap, more interested in company and conversation than I was in food. Maria, seeming to understand that, chattered at me as she prepared a tray for Sebastian. She asked me about Los Angeles, saying she had never seen a city so large; she had only been to Santa Fé three times in her life.

"You've been here a long while," I said.

"Yes. A long while." She sighed. "I came with the boys' mother. With Angelina."

"I saw her picture in the hall."

Maria frowned. "An empty thing, that painting. It doesn't show the true woman. A woman of the north. Very strong, for all her sweetness, very solid, and every promise made was every promise kept. I remember, she was just a girl, then, and I was too, but she said, 'Come with me, Maria. You'll be happy. You'll have your home.' And it was just as she said."

"But your family?" I asked softly.

Maria slid me a glance out of slanted dark eyes. "I was married for two years. He was young, a boy who lived in the past, and dreamed of it, and would not look at the future."

"You left him?"

Maria smiled sadly. "I left him in the cemetery." She paused, when she went on, the sweet foreign rhythm always present in her speech had become stronger. "He lost himself in the wine—muscat the curse—and one winter night going home to the Pueblo, he lost himself in the cold he couldn't feel." She paused again, and then, with a quick movement of her wrists, snapped a white napkin over Sebastian's tray. "There," she said. "And would you like to see my room?"

"Oh, yes, if you don't mind."

She flung back a door in the side wall. "You see? It is my home."

I stood there, entranced. Bright serapes were hung on the whitewashed walls. Indian woven rugs were on the floor. A row of *santos* carved of wood, time-scoured and old, graced the mantel.

"It's beautiful," I breathed.

"Angelina promised, you see."

Everywhere, scattered about the room, there were photographs, small and large, framed and unframed.

"May I look?" I asked.

She waved me in.

There was a faint pungent odor. She explained that it was piñon incense.

I touched one picture.

"Michael and Jamie," she told me. "And here—Annetta——" Maria put another framed snapshot into my hand.

Michael had been about twelve then, serious, tall. Jamie, grinning at eight, as he did now. Annetta, perhaps ten, smiled at me upside down in an efficient handstand.

"The rogues' gallery—they are lovely, Maria."

"My babies. My family," she answered softly, her plump lined face glowing with love.

I had to look away from her lest my eyes betray my shame. I, emptyhearted, an impostor, could be only humble before her devotion.

I moved quickly around the bright room, murmuring a word or two at each picture of Jamie, saying, "Michael, oh, yes, and here's Annetta again," sounding like any young wife when exposed to the family album, but I was relieved when I heard a discreet cough, and Henley called, "Maria, you inside?"

Maria turned so quickly that her full pleated skirt billowed like a dancer's costume, and, light as a dancer in her blue boots, she hurried to the kitchen.

I followed her, moving slowly. I closed the door carefully behind me, and the sweet incense scent disappeared. I hated to leave Maria's home, to return to the reality of Cromwell Crossing from what had seemed to me a place apart—a refuge.

"I forgot the coffee," Maria was telling Henley. With a quick smile at me, she went on. "It must be fresh and hot."

Henley waited. In a little while, Maria set a gleaming silver pot on the tray, and Henley carried it out.

"Now, your lunch, Robin," Maria told me.

"Oh, it doesn't matter. I'm not hungry."

She made a disapproving sound, and told me that I ate less than the bird after which I was named. By the time she had finished warning me that the mountains demanded good appetite, she had set a hamburger and salad in front of me.

"There," she told me, wiping her hands on her broad hips. "There. Now, eat."

I had just finished my lunch when I heard the car pull in.

"Annetta, Jamie," Maria said, smiling.

I felt myself freeze. The moment I had wanted to avoid had finally come as I had known it would. I wondered which of the various Jamie faces I would see.

Annetta's high excited voice preceded her. "I want to do it again tomorrow," she was saying. "Oh, what fun! A hundred miles, Jamie. You saw it yourself. And I'll bet I can get it up to a hundred and ten!"

"Driving," Maria mumbled under her breath, her smile gone. She turned to me, said quickly, "You tell him, Robin. He must not take her driving. He must not let her. Sebastian does not want to——" Maria stopped as the door crashed open.

Annetta bounded in, lithe in tight tan jeans and a white jersey. She grabbed Maria, hugged her, swung her around. "You know what we did? We took Jamie's car, me at the wheel, out on the highway, and we went flying, flying——"

Jamie grinned. "Tone it down, Annetta. You're making enough noise to awaken the dead."

"And also to worry Sebastian," Maria said tartly. "You know, Jamie—you know he doesn't want her to drive."

"Oh, old Sebastian always finds something to worry about. Annetta can drive a car, or tear one down and build one up, as good as I can any day. Ask Henley. He taught her, just as he taught me."

Maria started to say more, but Jamie shrugged, turned to me. "And how's my bride this fine morning?"

"Just fine. Had a sun bath, visited with Sebastian, read to him a bit, and——"

Annetta moaned, flung herself into a chair. "You read!

That book! The Cromwell Bible, I'll bet. 'And in 1848'. . . ."

I grinned at her. "It's old stuff to you, but it's new stuff to me."

"Sounds like you did okay," Jamie put in, giving me a conspiratorial wink. "And what about the war wound? Is it mending without strain?" He pulled my skirt above my knee. "The leg's still there, and nice, too."

I brushed my skirt down, said hastily, "It's all right," and added, "Maria showed me her room, and all the pictures of you and Annetta, and——"

I caught a glimpse of Annetta's face. All the glow had gone out of it, leaving it blank, the black jet eyes shining with malice. But as I watched, the glow came back. She blinked a smile into her eyes.

My voice had trailed away. I'd forgotten what I was talking about. Fortunately, no one noticed because Maria was asking if Annetta and Jamie had had lunch.

"Hot dogs in town," Annetta said gaily.

"Hot dogs," Maria grumbled. "They're not good for you."

"Maria, don't baby me!" Annetta objected loudly.

I asked, "What about that grand tour you promised me, Annetta? Could we do it now?"

She jumped up. "Of course. That's what we'll do. Come on, Jamie. Let's show Robin our castle."

I went with her, Jamie following us.

"You know the first floor," Annetta said, *"and* all the portraits *and* the planters and the terrace, so we'll go straight up." She chose the front stairs, then looked back to grin at Jamie. "North wing first, or south wing?"

"North," he said.

She paused at the entrance, patted a damask wall hanging. "And this?"

"Later," Jamie told her.

"Okay, later."

I asked what they were talking about, but Annetta went ahead, saying, "You'll see. It's a cute idea they had." She paused, flung open a door. "This was Sebastian's suite."

"It was a beautiful room once," Jamie said.

I could see what he meant. The furnishings were lovely, shining mahogany, a deep-blue rug, impressive paintings on the pale walls. But the air was dusty now, damp and cold.

"After Father got sick last year," Jamie explained, "he had the glass walls of the conservatory downstairs closed in, and moved down there."

Annetta moved back into the hall. "Come on. Let's go ahead." She started down the hall with Jamie and me just behind her.

We were passing another door, toward the end of the passage when Jamie said, "You're traveling pretty fast, aren't you?"

"Oh, I almost forgot," Annetta told him.

Jamie opened the door for me. It was a sitting room. A big piano filled one corner. Gold drapes hung at the tall windows. A gold love seat was pulled up before a fireplace.

"That's a nice room," I said.

"Ayren's," Annetta told me expressionlessly. "We never use it any more."

This time I was the one who backed out into the hall. I imagined that I felt a dank cool wind follow me.

There was an odd bend to the corridor. Annetta went around it, leaned against another damask wall hanging, with her arms folded across her chest.

"Now guess," she said. "What's behind here?"

"It could only be a door," I told her. "A secret passageway."

She looked disappointed, jerked the hanging aside. "Jamie told you," she mumbled.

"I didn't." He laughed. "You don't give Robin any credit for brains."

"I do," Annetta retorted. "I know she must be smart, else why would she have married you?"

"Why not?" Jamie chuckled.

I wished they would stop. Their voices sounded too shrill in the tiny stair well. I followed Annetta, beginning to feel as if the small steps would continue forever.

At last, we reached the top, a huge room of slanted eaves and crowded shadows.

"It used to be servants' quarters in the old days," Jamie explained. "Then Sebastian got the bright idea of ripping the walls out and making a recreation room for us kids." He bent over a dusty pool table to tumble a ball along torn green felt, and went on, pausing to kick a rocking horse into motion. "Yours, Annetta. Remember?"

"Oh, let's get out of here," his sister said. "Nurseries are out of style these days."

Jamie, rummaging by then at the end of the big room, looked up. "We'll show Robin the real nursery."

"It's not," Annetta snapped. "And, anyhow, I'm not——"

"I'm not a baby any more," Jamie whined in a mock falsetto.

But Annetta ignored him. She grinned at me. "We take these stairs down."

Another tiny passageway, another narrow door, another damask wall hanging. Out in the hall again, I realized that we were just opposite my suite.

"It crosses the whole house," Annetta said, delighted with my obvious surprise. "And, except for Michael's suite, and yours, there's nothing else at this end but my rooms." She went dancing ahead of us to fling back the door.

I stood there, admiring, but wondering, too. The sitting room was gold and green, with polished cherry furniture and stacks of satin cushions in all the corners. The bedroom was furnished with a huge pink-and-white canopied bed, a white dresser, and a hairy white rug on the floor.

Admiring, but wondering, too, I said, "This is lovely, Annetta."

"Do you think so?" She paused deliberately. "To tell you the truth, I think it's awful. Ayren did it. And when she did, she had herself in mind. Don't you just see me in that bed?"

I grinned at her. "I had an idea, you know."

"Sure," Jamie chuckled. "You started looking for the baseball bat that wasn't in the corner, and the horse turd that wasn't on the rug."

Annetta made a great point of ignoring him. "But anyhow," she said to me, "I do have a marvelous view. The bedroom window faces west—to Los Angeles. And the sitting room window faces south—to Las Vegas."

Jamie tugged at a fistful of her dark curls. "Savage, didn't they teach you anything about geography in those ten schools they threw you out of?"

"Just the same amount as they taught you," Annetta retorted. She flung herself down on a sofa. "There's lots more, Robin, all kinds of nooks and crannies, but you get Jamie to show them to you."

"Not me," Jamie protested. "After all, I've lost track."

"If you hadn't gone away, you'd know lots of things," Annetta told him smugly. "Your trouble is you don't have good sense."

Jamie laughed. "My trouble is I want a quiet corner and some small peace, and with my big-mouth sister around, I doubt that I'll ever find it."

"Peace and quiet? In this house?" Annetta snorted.

I knew that she was joking, but somehow, to me, her words seemed serious.

Chapter *TEN*

A FEW DAYS later, the four of us were at breakfast together—Annetta, Michael, Jamie, and me.

"Today is the day I'll show you the caves," Annetta told me.

Maria turned from the stove. "Annetta, you are too old to go in the caves now."

"But I want her to see." She grinned at me appealingly. "Bobby, why is it that I'm always too old for something, or too young for something?"

"And that's enough of that 'Bobby' stuff," Michael put in.

Though I was glad he had reminded her, I started to say that I didn't mind; however, Michael frowned me into silence.

Annetta shrugged and returned to her original train of thought. "But it's a perfect day for the caves."

"Robin's leg should be healed first," Michael said firmly.

Jamie leaned forward to pat my cheek. "It is. She's a sturdy one, she is," he said with mock fondness. A fondness which I knew appeared genuine to the others. For the past few days, he had played the part of loving husband with a zest I found almost embarrassing.

I tipped my head away from him, said, "Oh, my leg's all right now. Unless I bump it. And of course, you know how sore thumbs are——"

106

"See, she wants to go," Annetta cried.

"Better wait," Michael insisted.

Annetta flashed me a quick glance. "Robin, you decide."

But Michael didn't give me a chance. He said, "No," with so much firmness that I didn't think it a good idea to contradict him.

"Then what will we do?" Annetta demanded sulkily. "You're always upstairs fiddling with your papers, and talking on the phone as if your life depended on it. And if you're not doing that then you're wandering around like a lost sheep. And Jamie——" Her face suddenly cleared. "I know what! I'll teach Robin shooting."

That time I said "No" just as firmly as Michael had before. I was afraid of guns, didn't like them, and playing with them was not my idea of recreation.

"Then what?"

"Play chess with Sebastian," Jamie suggested, with a chuckle.

"Go soak your head," Annetta retorted.

Maria, softly, said, "You like to play chess, Annetta."

"Before everybody came home," Annetta pouted. "But, now——" She shrugged. "Oh, I give up. What a family!"

"Amen," Jamie grinned.

But Annetta *hadn't* given up.

Later, when I was on the balcony, studying the valley below, she came up, giving me a conspiratorial grin.

"You must be sick of looking at the view. Let's go, Robin. Do you have slacks? If not, I'll lend you some of mine."

"Go where?"

"On a very dangerous trek," she said in a whisper, smiling. "Cave hunting——"

"But they said——"

Annetta shrugged. "We don't have to listen, do we?"

I didn't really think I'd enjoy climbing around inside the mountain, but I didn't want to rebuff Annetta. Besides, she was right. Just because Michael spoke didn't mean that I had to listen.

"I have some jeans," I told her. "Wait while I change."

She followed me into the bedroom, curled on the bed while I put on blue jeans and a shirt.

"This is going to be fun." She grinned.

She led me outside, then along the balcony to the place it turned the corner and became a flight of steps that led to the ground level. Hers was, I realized, the corner room, a window on the balcony, another, a few feet above the steps.

She told me to wait outside while she went in for flashlights. In a moment, she was back. She handed a torch to me and said, "Now, away we go!"

Annetta went ahead, chattering over her shoulder, leading me up the steep red slope behind the house. We moved through channeled cliffs and huge fluted boulders. I clambered along, trying to keep up, but, gradually, she pulled ahead, though I could still hear her kicking up stones and whistling as she went. I followed a trail, no more than a stream-hollowed ditch between walls of roughened clay, until it emerged on a high narrow ridge.

Annetta was waiting for me. "Look how far we've already come," she cried.

I glanced down. The house was far below us, a gray stone mass sprawled on its shelf, faintly edged with haze drifting up from the valley. Bits of reflected sun glimmered at me from the windows. Leaves danced along the pitched roof. In spite of their tiny movements, the building seemed wrapped in absolute stillness, an abandoned place on the brink of final decay.

I shivered. "It's a long way down. No wonder I'm so breathless."

I hooked the flashlight to my belt so that both my hands would be free.

When Annetta asked, "Ready?" I nodded agreement. She grinned. "Your leg doesn't hurt, does it?"

"I'm fine."

She started along the ridge. I gave the crouching house below a last look as I followed her, moving still further up the mountainside, gradually circling higher and higher, until the ridge faded away to nothing and, above us, I saw slits of shadowed darkness against the craggy red.

"Here's the work," Annetta said, pointing up at the fissures. "We go in through there. But it takes hands and feet to do it. Maria's people might have lived in these caves once, Robin. A long, long time ago. You ask Sebastian. He'll tell you." She paused. "Sometimes, when I'm here alone, I pretend I can still hear them." She stretched, reaching for handholds and footholds, clambered up, and clung, seemingly to thin air. Then she called down to me, "You can do it, can't you?"

I nodded assent, wondering if I really could, but determined to try. I heaved myself up, clawing with fingers and toes; finally, I felt the wide rim with my groping hand and Annetta's fingers curled around my wrist to help me with a last pull that drew me up and in. Gasping, I flung myself down. My leg had begun to throb, bruised, stung into pain, by that last inching climb.

I managed to grin at Annetta, "Few minutes rest is in order," I panted.

The girl curled up beside me. "But not too long," she warned. "If you wait, you stiffen up; then it's murder to get started again."

I looked around. We were in a shallow rounded area. The opening to the outside was barely wide enough for us to have snaked our way through. It allowed a filtering of pale light by which I could see the dry scaly curves of low walls.

"There's a lot of other ways in, of course," Annetta said, proud as a tour guide, "but I didn't want you to have to climb too far."

"The climb was quite far enough."

"This is just an outside chamber," Annetta went on. "The guards in olden times probably kept watch from here. Back there, inside——" Annetta pointed, "——the real caves begin."

She uncurled with a swift lithe movement. "We'd better go on now."

Still breathing hard, I too rose.

"Don't bump your head," she warned. "I'll go first."

Half-crouched, she moved around me, stepped from the false twilight of filtered sun into darkness. Then, her shadow slightly darker than the black around her, she straightened up and moved on, her voice trailing back to me. "See—the caves—they're all around us. They wind up and down, they're connected by tunnels in every direction like honeycombs."

I snapped on the flashlight. It threw a narrow yellow beam that outlined Annetta's slender body and threw beyond it a grotesque moving shadow.

"Don't use your flash unless you absolutely have to," she called back. "You can run the battery dead."

I turned off the light, blinking against gray darkness. The tunnel opened into a small chamber.

From the other side of it, Annetta waved at me. "Come on, Robin," she shouted. "Don't hang back so much."

As she disappeared, I stumbled toward her.

The darkness faded under wisps of thin light that drained in through tiny overhead openings.

I had nearly caught up to her, ready to call it quits,

when Annetta dodged into another tunnel, laughing. "Are you there, Robin?"

"I'm here. Yes, I'm here. But wait, Annetta," I called.

And the echoes came back. "Are you there, Robin?" mixed with laughter. And then, "I'm here. Yes, I'm here. But wait, Annetta." Rolling, whispering echoes mixed with laughter, gradually faded away.

I ran, followed her through winding dark labyrinths, switching the flashlight on and off. Its dim yellow beam seemed to glow more brightly as I went on. Water slick glinted on the black walls—a slow whisper of endless drops pattering on ungiving rock.

I ran, splashed through puddles, tripped, and fell, and forced myself to rise, trying to keep up with her. But Annetta was always ahead, calling back to me, describing things I couldn't see.

"Wait, Annetta!" I yelled again breathlessly.

"I'm here," she shouted. "Just keep on coming. I'm here."

But, all around me, I thought I heard echoes, footsteps, the swift menacing sound of tumbling stones, and that slow steady whisper of dripping water.

I plunged on, really frightened, but chiding myself for letting the strange atmosphere inside the mountain get the better of me, and wishing that I, too, had Annetta's cat's eyes so that I could find my way without touching the slimy walls.

Then the tunnel became a small dim room. At its far wall, there were three blurred openings.

I paused, yelling: "Annetta, where are you? I can't see your light!"

"Come on," my tormentor cried. "I'm here."

I hesitated, then tore on following the sound of her voice. But I hit my head on a low rock overhang. I went down to my hands and knees, shivering, dizzy. I realized that I had dropped the flashlight. I groped for it, straining to see in the empty dark.

There was a moment of blank silence. I heard faint ghostly footsteps again, and the slow steady whisper of water.

Then Annetta called: "Robin! Bobby! Bobby, where are you?"

I shouted. "Here, Annetta! Wait until I find my flash."

At that moment, my searching hand touched it, my fingers closed compulsively around its cold grip. I pushed myself up and followed its dim yellow beam into an opening.

I rushed on heedlessly, shouting, "Wait, wait!" Staring ahead into the dim light of the flash, I blundered into a solid wall, and then I tripped and fell flat.

The flashlight beam made a wild swinging arc, dancing up and down in the shadows. The torch then fell out of my numb hand and went spinning and whirling away leaving faint trails of light that faded to nothing in a tinkle of broken glass, tortured metal, and a distant splash.

Those sounds were mingled in my ears with my own scream of terror. For that faint trail of light, before it died, had briefly touched a shadowed alcove like a niche in a church. There, I had seen the flesh-stripped corpse of a woman, a grinning skull, a sprawl of fabric once pink, frivolous high-heeled slippers.

Still screaming, I scrambled up. With the light gone, I could see nothing. But the scene was etched in horrific acid in my mind. I dashed forward wildly, tripping once again over the suitcase that had tumbled me before to the wet rock, kicking it aside, and going on.

With my hands over my face, plunging into empty darkness, I fled.

Chapter *ELEVEN*

FOOTSTEPS seemed to pursue me. Somewhere ahead, in the dark, Annetta's clear young voice called, "Robin! Oh, Bobby, where are you?" The words returned again and again in long mocking echoes. I stumbled on blindly, terrified beyond thought, weeping, my hands outstretched for my fingertips must serve as my eyes.

It could have been only moments from the time that I stumbled into the alcove to discover that pitiful tangle of putrefying flesh and cloth. I had turned away, frantic, to circle in the dark. But it seemed like endless hours, my ears full of the clatter and rumble of distorted sound, my breath burning my throat. Then hands came out of the shadows. Hands touched me, caught me, held me fast.

I choked out an anguished scream, imagining the grip of skeletal fingers, imagining that the tangle of bone and rotted flesh had risen to pursue me.

My cry was smothered by a hard warm hand pressed across my mouth. There was a sudden hush as the echoes around me died. I heard my own hard breath, and another's. A low harsh voice whispered, "It's me, Michael, Robin. Can you be still?"

I could feel a living heart pound against my breast. Was it his heart or mine? I could feel myself tremble inside the circle of his arms. Or was Michael trembling too?

At last, he asked again, "Can you be still, Robin?" and I managed a nod against his gagging hand. It slid away from my lips, leaving a chill where there had been warmth.

Michael shouted ahead to Annetta, "Stand there, Annetta. Don't move. Do you hear me? There are pits and falls. Robin's nearly been hurt. Just stand until I come to you. Do you hear me?"

Her answering shout came faintly. "Michael! Where are you?"

"We'll come to you. Just wait."

His arms were still around me. I leaned against him, secure within their circling strength. I turned my cheek to his chest.

"All right now?" Michael asked gently.

I nodded, and he moved back. His arms dropped away. My whole body felt suddenly cold again. I shivered.

"What happened, Robin?" he asked quietly.

I found it hard to speak through my numb lips. "Michael, I didn't dream it—I saw it—a body, back there. That's when the flash dropped and I ran——"

His taut whisper stopped me. "A *body*, Robin? Where?"

"I'll show you."

Michael moved and I was briefly blinded by a sudden flowering of light. I knew he was convinced by the glimpse he had had of my face.

"Show me," he said.

And faintly again, Annetta cried, "Hurry up, Michael. I'm not going to stand here all day. What's wrong?"

"You wait!" he shouted. "We're coming." And to me, "Quickly, Robin. Where?"

"Somewhere here, an alcove—it can't be far——"

I felt the tautness in him, felt it through the grip he

had on my arm. He was hurting me and I told him so. He apologized tonelessly, but he didn't let go.

I tried to describe it. "There were three openings—all dark. I didn't know which way Annetta had gone. I chose one, and then ran, and——" Trying to visualize it again in my mind, seeing it, made my voice quaver.

"Yes," Michael said quickly. "Yes, I heard you run." He snapped the flash on, swung a pale beam around the damp walls, heightened the black of the grotesque shadows, and picked out an opening where I saw the faint glint of dripping water.

"I felt waterdrops. And when I dropped my light it made a splash, Michael."

"Then we'll go that way." He went first. "Hold me, Robin."

I wanted to touch Michael, and I didn't want to. I reached out, yet held back. His hand came groping, touched my shoulder, slid down my arm, leaving a trail of warmth, to my fingers. He folded my fingers around his belt. "Hold tight, now." And he laughed softly. "Thank God you're not a sniveler, Robin."

I didn't answer. I followed, feeling as if I'd had a medal of honor bestowed, but knowing I didn't deserve it. Knowing, too, that he had seen the marks of tears on my cheeks, had touched them when he'd grabbed me and covered my mouth to keep me from screaming.

We went very slowly. I gasped as a cold drop hit my forehead when we stepped through the opening. The flash went on again. We were in a small chamber, a pitted gray room. A few yards ahead of us, a tunnel yawned. The light swung back and forth as we moved through it.

My knees were weak again. I saw two familiar black openings. "One of those," I whispered.

"We'll try." The light went off. "Hold on, Robin."

As if I needed to be told! My fingers were frozen on

Michael's belt. He was my only contact with reality. I didn't dare let go.

We went on. He kicked something, stumbled, caught himself. I nearly fell, but managed to cling to him, like a papoose on his back.

"Yes, here, Michael. I remember the suitcase. That's when I fell, and then——"

The faint light went on. I couldn't see around him, but I heard his shocked gasp.

Michael came to a full stop, paralyzed, and I stumbled into him. I knew he had seen the corpse which had sent me screaming away through the dark.

The light went off. I felt Michael turn, then his arms came around me.

"It's there," he said in a hoarse voice. "Yes, Robin, it's really there." And then, "Could Annetta have seen this?"

"No. I don't see how. She wasn't in here, Michael. I missed her somehow, and——"

He cut in, his voice harsh. "Listen, Robin. We don't have much time. This is Annetta's mother here. Do you understand me? *It's Rose.* We mustn't tell Annetta. Not a word to her."

"But you can't leave a woman here like this. Unburied and unmourned. Michael, you can't——"

"I can't do anything else, Robin. We mustn't ever tell anyone what we've found. Nobody can know. Because of Annetta. And because of Sebastian too. Don't you see? He thinks Rose ran away, made a new life for herself. It would kill him to discover that she lay here, rotting, so close to him. It would kill him to find out she died in a crazy accident, while he——"

"But how?" I protested. "Michael, why would she come here, and why——"

"It doesn't matter." He gave me a little shake, his arms tight. "It was a long time ago. You must forget you have seen this. We'll make it *our* secret. Robin, can I trust you?"

I nodded agreement, wondering what he would have done if I told him I wouldn't keep the secret of the cave.

"We'll have to go to Annetta now."

"But it's horrible, Michael. Just to turn our backs——"

"Do what I say," he told me with such finality that I didn't dare argue any more. "Promise me, Robin."

"All right, Michael. I promise."

He let go of me. He hooked my fingers through his belt. "We'll get Annetta."

He lit the flash briefly, then clicked it off as he went first, drawing me from the alcove with him. Without hesitation, he chose another opening and stepped through.

"Michael, how did you happen to find me?" I asked. "How did you know——?"

He grunted. "I know the caves almost as well as Annetta."

"But how did you know——?"

"Maria saw the two of you taking off." Then, "Save your breath, Robin."

We stepped into pale light that dribbled in from overhead.

Michael paused, looked around, then called, "Annetta, are you there?"

In the distance, we heard her shout, "Why are you so long?"

Moments later, we saw the flash beams moving at a corner, and then she was there, laughing. "Honestly, you oughtn't to fall back so, Robin. Michael! what on earth are you doing here?"

"That was a thoroughly stupid thing to do," Michael told her coldly. "Robin doesn't know her way around these caves the way we do. The moment you were out of sight, she was completely lost."

"Oh, Robin, I am sorry," Annetta said contritely.

"You *are* a mess, aren't you? Oh, dear, what a real beast I am. I never dreamed. Look, you didn't really get lost, did you? You weren't really scared?"

"No," I said weakly. "Not really."

"Why then, why were you racing around screaming? For goodness sake, I thought there were ghosts chasing you. And then Michael yelled for me to stand still, and it took you so long, and I——"

Michael interrupted. "Robin's worn out. It's time we headed out of here."

"But I thought she'd enjoy the caves. I didn't think she'd——"

I said quickly, "Maybe we can do it another time."

"Never," Michael said firmly. "This is your first and last visit to the Cromwell caves. As for you, Annetta, it's your last one, too. If I catch you catfooting around inside the mountain again, I'm going to wallop you. And if you don't believe me, just try it and see."

"Oh, all right," Annetta said sullenly. "I believe you."

I believed him, too. I was relieved that she didn't argue.

In a few minutes, we were outside. I was amazed to see the sun still high, the sky a sharp painful blue. It seemed to me that I had been within the terrifying walls of the mountain for days. Then I thought of Rose, lying there alone forever.

I shivered.

Michael's fingers curled around my arm. "All right?"

"Of course," I said steadily.

The white flash of his engaging smile quickly brought an unaccustomed tenderness to his face.

Michael stopped on a high ridge. "Wait, Robin, let me see." He went down. Beyond his shoulder, far below, I could see the misty outlines of the house.

"You've torn the bandage off your leg. We'll have to replace it."

I glanced down. The knees of my jeans were in tatters. My sandals were torn. I looked as if I had fallen into a pit and climbed out leaving skin behind me. All at once, I felt each small burn and sting.

Michael rose, the tenderness gone from his face. "Annetta, you don't have to tell Sebastian that Robin was so nearly lost. It would only worry him."

"Sure. Why would I tell him?" Annetta agreed, flinging back her dark curls. "It wasn't anything anyhow." She grinned at me, more child than woman. "Now you've seen the Cromwell caves, at least."

I knew that she couldn't realize what those terrifying moments had been to me. She didn't know that her mother's body lay there, entombed in the mountain, her fleshless skull grinning forever into darkness, high-heeled slippers near the faded remnants of a pink dress.

As far as Annetta was concerned, we had been on a lark, a slightly scary one, like a roller-coaster ride in an amusement area.

We trudged down the mountainside in silence. At the house, Michael said, "Go in through the kitchen."

Indoors, Maria, polishing a copper pot looked up, a welcoming smile on her face which died when she saw me. She cried, "Robin, what is it? What has happened?"

Michael said quickly, "It's okay, Maria."

Annetta threw herself into a kitchen chair. "Boy, am I bushed! We have been round and round inside the mountain, and round and round outside again, and——"

"You are too old to go in the caves," Maria said severely.

"I'm too old to go in the caves, and I'm too young to be let alone," Annetta protested sullenly.

"But——"

"She's not going any more," Michael said. "She promised me, Maria."

Maria's somber eyes flicked at my face, then slid away. "Sebastian asked for you."

I went to the door. "I'll clean up before I go in." I managed to smile. "Don't I need it?"

She gave me a sudden bright smile in return. "Robin, small as a bird—but birds have the great talent; they know how to fly."

Wondering what she meant, I glanced at Michael. His face was suddenly rock-hard, his dark brows angling in a frown over his curtained pale eyes.

It was only upstairs when I sat before the mirror that I realized just how I looked. My face was drawn, hollowed out by fear. My hair was wet, matted, streaked with red clay. My eyes glittered a feverish green. The tears of fright had left trails on my cheeks. My blue jeans and shirt were torn, stained, damp. My elbows and knees were marked with a dozen small cuts and bruises. The bandage on my shin had come loose. I jerked it off completely.

I showered quickly and dressed in a skirt and blouse. I put a fresh narrow piece of adhesive over a tiny gauze pad across my shin. Back at the mirror, I forced a smile to my lips. It would be a good idea to practice that smile a bit before I went down to Sebastian.

I hoped I would be able to pretend nothing had happened. It wouldn't be easy. For it had occurred to me graphically that once again I had been in danger. I could have been lost like Rose was. I could have gone stumbling on alone within those dark tunnels until, at last, I fell— I died—and no one would have known.

I wondered why Michael had followed when Maria told him where Annetta and I had gone.

Yet, no matter how I turned it over in my mind, I still couldn't see how the near accident in the cave could have been anything more than an odd coincidence. The sort of odd coincidence that happens in life.

I was putting on lipstick when Jamie came in.

"I've been busy at work on the old man," he said.

"And?"

Come for
the filter...

© Lorillard 1975

A PRODUCT OF *Lorillard*

KENT
WITH
THE FAMOUS MICRONITE FILTER

DELUXE LENGTH

18 mg. "tar," 1.2 mg. nicotine av. per cigarette, FTC Report Oct. '74.

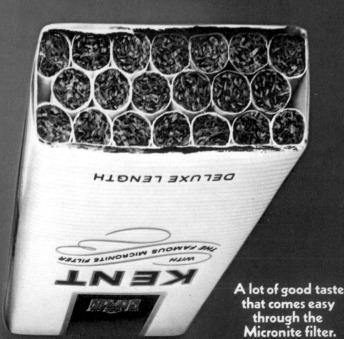

© Lorillard 1975

...you'll stay for the taste.

A lot of good taste that comes easy through the Micronite filter.

"I knew it would take a while. You've sold him all right. Now I have to do the same."

"I'm glad you finally realized that."

Jamie's boyish grin faded. "You don't help much by sneaking away with Annetta. Some sweet little loving bride——"

"I'm sorry. I guess I shouldn't have," I said. And I was sincere. I wished I hadn't gone with Annetta to the caves. I wished I'd never seen the broken body which lay alone in a forgotten alcove.

"Not that it matters." Jamie stretched out on the bed, folded his arms behind his head, his light-blue eyes following me curiously. Then, with that peculiar sensitivity I'd observed in him before, he demanded, "What's the matter, Robin?"

"Nothing," I told him.

He grinned again. "Just concentrate on what you'll do when we leave here," he said thinly. "Think about those emeralds in the drawer."

I didn't answer him. I didn't want to think about the emeralds, nor about the new life I would make when Jamie and I finally parted company after we left Cromwell Crossing. I was remembering how I had felt within the circle of Michael's arms, the feel of my cheek against his chest, how our two hearts had seemed for long moments to beat together.

Jamie drawled, "If you're going down now, do your act good for Sebastian."

"Oh, leave me alone," I cried.

"What did I say to bring that on?" Jamie chuckled.

Michael was at the window, hands jammed in his pockets, his wide shoulders rigid.

I knew he was there to stop me if I should say the wrong thing. But I had promised him not to tell Sebastian about the gruesome body I had found inside the mountain, and, looking at Sebastian leaning back in the easy chair, his gaunt faced lined, his lips bluish, I knew I had to keep that promise.

I hesitated there in the doorway.

Sebastian raised his head. "Come in, girl. Sit with us," and then, with a chuckle, "I hear you've been traipsing around the countryside with Annetta."

Michael swung around, his pale eyes narrowed, staring at me from beyond Sebastian's shoulder.

"We had a good walk," I said carefully. Overly aware of the moment's waiting silence, I made myself grin. "I think this is the most beautiful place in the world, Sebastian." I realized as the words came out that I had spoken the truth. The valley below, the mountains, the arching sky, had somehow laid soothing hands upon my heart.

Michael's taut face softened briefly. "I might as well get some work done," he said and went out.

Sebastian looked pleased. "I'm glad you like the high country, Robin."

"Anybody would."

"Anybody—except Jamie," Sebastian said softly. "And speaking of him—where has he gone?"

"I left him upstairs."

"Sleeping." Sebastian sighed.

"Oh, no. Not sleeping."

"Then daydreaming. Daydreaming about how he's going to spend my money. *My* money!"

I didn't know what to say.

"You explain it to me, Robin. If you can. I've got two sons. One knows his own name, and the other doesn't want to. Now how does that happen?"

"It must be hard for Michael to do his work—I mean —whatever it is that has to be done—from here——"

Sebastian allowed himself to be diverted momentarily. "We always did do it from here. Right from that desk where you're sitting like a true robin on a bough. That desk was the capital of the kingdom." He grinned to let me know he was joking. "That was until I turned sick. Until the trouble came." His voice slowed even more. "I reckon Michael doesn't have much else to concentrate on these days except the work."

"Will he stay here long?"

Sebastian shrugged. "As long as he wants to, I guess. He can always fly down to Austin for a few days. As a matter of fact, we were just talking of that when you came in." Sebastian's face brightened. "If he does, you give him those green stones of yours, and he'll get them made into earrings. You got holes in your ears or not?"

I shook my head.

"His mother did," Sebastian said. "And Ayren, too."

I wished longingly that I had pierced ears.

"Anyhow, you tell him what you want, and he'll get it done for you."

"There's no hurry."

"Why, girl, you might as well be wearing them. I don't believe pretties should be hidden away. Unless——" he grinned at me, "unless as an investment, of course."

My face got hot. I wondered if he were thinking that I wanted to keep the stones intact so that I could sell them later.

Sebastian's voice changed. "If Jamie'd settle down, and grab hold as he should, then Michael would go on back to Austin for good, I reckon. It's not easy for him here."

"I guess not," I said.

I wondered if that were what kept that strange hard look on Michael's face—as if he were seeing Ayren in the shadows of the sad old manor.

"No, not easy. I've been through it. I understand. When his mother died——"

I realized that was the second time Sebastian had said—— "his mother" referring to Michael. Not "the boys' mother." I saw how, in small ways, unthinking ways, Jamie had been subtly hurt.

Sebastian sighed. "Yes, that was a blow. To all of us. Jamie came squalling into this world, screaming for his mother who had left it as he cried for her, screaming for my poor Angelina who couldn't answer, and I guess he's been screaming for her ever since, one way and another. And there was Michael, all of four, not understanding his loss. Yes, a blow for all of us. A man has a lot of them in his life, I guess."

"Michael must have loved Ayren very much," I said, aware of a strange ache in my chest.

"She was his wife, Robin," Sebastian said simply.

I slid off the desk. I knew I had to get away from Sebastian before I cried.

Chapter TWELVE

THAT EVENING Jamie was restless. He had insisted that I go outside with him after dinner. He paced the terrace, swearing under his breath, as he dragged me along beside him in a miserable tigerish stride.

"What's the matter with you?" I demanded.

He tilted his head to look up at the stars. "You know, don't you?"

I shook my head.

"All my life, I've been doing just what I'm doing now."

"If you can't be patient, Jamie———"

He swore softly again. "What do you think I *am* being?"

"I've done the best I could, Jamie."

His face became boyish again. "Sure you have, Robin. We just have to give it more time, I guess. Sebastian's bound to get tired of trying to outwait me."

I was too conscious of the shadow on the porch—the tall straight motionless shadow. I was certain it was Michael watching us.

Jamie said, "I've got to get out of here. I'll go into town."

He started ahead of me. I hurried to catch up.

"I'll go too," I offered, not wanting to be left alone in the house.

"I'd rather be alone," Jamie told me.

"In that case——" But I let the words trail away. We had reached the porch by then. I didn't want Michael to hear Jamie and me quarreling.

Jamie, aware of that, I was sure, grinned at me and drawled, "See you later, Robin," and, to Michael, "Keep an eye on my wife."

Moments later I heard him whistling at the door before it slammed behind him. I started to go in. Michael stopped me.

"Wait, Robin. I wanted to thank you."

I knew what he meant—I had not let Sebastian guess about my fright in the cave, nor told him about Rose's corpse.

"I don't want to hurt Sebastian," I said slowly. "But Michael, how can you pretend? There are things that have to be done."

He cut in, his shadowy face suddenly cold, frightening. "We won't talk about it. Not now. Not ever. It's between us, Robin, between us and only us. I trust you to keep it that way. If I didn't——"

When I tried to speak, he stopped me. "No, Robin. We have to forget it."

I realized that he wasn't pleading with me. He wasn't asking me to help. He was simply ordering me to do as he said.

"Do you really think I can forget?" I inquired.

"You have to."

I left Michael standing there and went up to my room. A little later, I heard him climb the steps slowly. He had told me to forget, but that was impossible. Rose's decaying body lay alone, lost forever, in the caves, where I had myself by a frightening coincidence also been so nearly lost forever.

A shiver went over me. I found myself sitting tensely on the edge of the green lounge, listening to the night sounds take over the stillness surrounding the old house.

My injured leg began to throb. All the accumulated bruises and cuts I had garnered in the cave began to ache. I wondered what was going to happen next. What would happen before Jamie was able to convince Sebastian that he deserved the same settlement that Michael had received.

I heard Annetta in the hallway, and Michael's toneless voice answering her. I was relieved when she knocked at my door. I hadn't wanted to be alone. I called for her to come in. She did, grinning at me.

"I just got the heave ho there." Annetta jerked her thumb over her shoulder toward Michael's door. "I thought I'd ask if you're okay."

"Of course, I am. Want to come in?"

"Just for a minute. I'm going down to play chess with Sebastian." Her shining eyes roved over the room.

I hoped Jamie and I had been careful enough to leave no sign that we occupied separate rooms.

"You're a sport," Annetta said abruptly. "I'm sorry

about this morning. I guess I love the caves and feel so at home in them that I just didn't think."

"Forget it," I told her, meaning it.

But I was unable to forget it, and that night, I stumbled through dark tunnels in my dreams, and an eerie shadow in a pink skirt stumbled after me.

Towards the end of the week, we all went down to the Robards' for dinner. It was Sebastian's first time away from home in months. I hadn't realized the extent of his weakness until, going with him to the car, I saw that he trembled with exhaustion.

I took his arm. "Let's rest here for a minute."

He nodded at me, not speaking, obviously saving his breath.

Michael maneuvered us into the car—the three of us, Sebastian and me with him, while Jamie and Annetta went with Henley in the second car. I wondered if the separation was deliberate on Michael's part.

Sebastian dozed in the back as we went slowly down the mountainside under a spectacular sunset.

Michael said, "This is the first time since you went down to the Robards' for stitching up that you've been away from the castle."

I agreed with him in surprise.

"It's a dull life Jamie has brought you to."

"Dull?"

"No gadding about. No nightclubs, no dancing, no——"

I said stiffly, "You probably have an exaggerated idea of my life in Los Angeles. When I say I was a model, you all think of those smart women in the magazines." I smiled at him. "I don't qualify. I'm more in the class of a salesgirl walking around in clothing I'd never be able to afford than I am a fashion model, you know."

"But you must have done something with your time."

"I must have," I assented. I went on, describing exactly how I had lived. The alarm clock that wakened me, the time clock I punched on my way into the outlet and punched again on my way out, the meals in the drugstore, the socializing I really didn't want, the emptiness of dates with men who didn't matter to me.

As I spoke, I realized the depths of my bitterness. I hadn't known how strongly I had disliked my former life. And I saw that it wasn't money that I had missed, but sincere emotional contacts.

Michael glanced at me sideways. "I wouldn't have expected you to feel that way," he said gently.

"Why not?"

He shrugged and didn't answer.

"And what about you?" I asked. "It must be difficult for you here—so far from———"

"If a man has his work, he doesn't need much else."

There was a soft chuckle from the back seat. Sebastian had been listening unashamedly. "Is that right, son?"

A grin touched Michael's mouth and instantly fled. "We won't argue about it, Sebastian."

"We will," Sebastian said. "He needs his work, and a woman too, and a place to belong in."

The dead silence was painful.

Michael's bitter chuckle didn't make it easier. "The Cromwell philosophy in a nutshell," he said tonelessly.

"It sounds good to me," I said, laughing, as if I hadn't heard the raw sound of pain in his voice.

Our few hours at the Robards' were pleasant. Sebastian was gay in his quiet way, Annetta full of sweetness, and Jamie high-spirited. Only Michael was withdrawn as usual.

I wondered if he also were remembering the niche in the mountain.

Before we left, Uncle Ned insisted that he check my

leg. When he saw the fresh bandage, he frowned, "Why did you take the other one off?"

"It fell off," I said.

His face cleared. "Well, let's see." And then he grinned. "Fine. You feeling brave? It will take about two weeks and some to heal. I'll get the stitches out right now."

"I'll come back tomorrow," I protested.

"You won't have to, except for a social visit." He bent his big head, moved his hands, mumbling, "Snip, snip, snip." And then, "Now that's a good job for a pretty girl, I'll guarantee you. Have a look."

"All done?"

"All done." He grinned. "Now we can go back and join the others."

As I went with him across the tree-sheltered patio, Uncle Ned asked, "How are things going up there, Robin?"

"Oh, fine," I answered.

"Fine—" He mimicked at me, his askew face gentle. "Now, Robin, I mean, what's Jamie going to do?"

"I don't know yet."

Uncle Ned shook his head.

Belinda came bustling to the door to meet us. "They went ahead. Sebastian was tiring so Michael drove him and Henley back."

"But Sebastian's all right?" I asked, suddenly anxious.

"Why, goodness, child, of course, he is. And if he weren't, I wouldn't have let him go. He's just grand, had a better time this night than I can remember when, but he does get tired. That's to be expected. Ask the doctor here."

"Maybe we'd better get back too," I said.

But after I'd gotten in the car with Jamie and Annetta, I realized they had other ideas. They decided to stop in the café on Main Street.

I protested, but Annetta said sulkily, "Well, we've got to do something."

Jamie added, "It won't be long. Just for a couple of beers."

The place was small, grimy, dim, crowded with informally dressed locals who gave us unfriendly stares and made mocking comments about the "high and mighty Cromwells" in deliberately loud whispers.

It was more than a couple of beers, and we stayed longer than I cared to. Yet Jamie ignored me when I said I wanted to leave. At last, the lights were turned off, and Jamie allowed me to persuade him that closing time was the time to go home.

Annetta was giggly on several beers, but Jamie was sullen.

"Now, you've got the picture of our night life," he told me, "you can go beering in town, or go beering in town."

I didn't want to argue with him, so I didn't answer. We fled up the mountain road under the stars.

The house was dark—a huge crouching figure surrounded by darker trees. When we went inside, I felt those waves of melancholy, that threat, the sadness, reach out to touch me with cold prickles on my skin. Now I knew that what I felt within Cromwell Crossing was more than sensitivity to my own guilt in being there. My deeds had not pitched a heavy stone planter down at me, nor led Rose to a lonely death in a mountain cave.

We climbed the stairs together. Annetta went off to her room, Jamie and I to our suite. I heard a door close and knew, without looking, that it had been Michael, waiting for us, watching again. I fell asleep finally, remembering the black terror of the cave, and thinking of Michael.

The next day, at breakfast, Annetta announced that she and Jamie were going out.

"You, Jamie," Maria demanded, "will you take her driving again?"

"Why not?" Annetta pouted. "I like to fly."

"But slowly, slowly," Maria pleaded. "You are not supposed to fly. And Sebastian worries, and——"

Jamie laughed, wrapped her plump form in his arms until she cried out. "Who worries? You, Maria? Or Sebastian?"

"We both," she admitted promptly, but her dark eyes were smiling now, full of love.

"And if we get into trouble, there's Henley to get us out of it, the way he always has," Jamie went on.

"No trouble," Maria said quickly. "Promise me. You will not go too fast, Jamie."

"Not too fast," he agreed, grinning, teasing her.

"Just a hundred and twenty," Annetta shouted.

Maria mumbled reproaches as they went out together. I watched them, wondering where Michael had gone.

I was curled up on the green lounge, looking at the sky when I heard the firm, limping steps that I knew were Michael's. I straightened up.

"Get over yesterday morning's excursion okay?" Michael asked.

I nodded.

"You look as if you need some rest."

"I do?"

His pale eyes were expressionless, his mouth hard. He stared at me for a moment. Then he said, "You don't sleep well in this house."

"How can I?"

He shrugged that away. "Robin, I'm not your enemy, you know."

It was odd that I wanted so much to believe him. Yet I knew he must be; he had to be if he knew the truth. He and Sebastian were on one side. Jamie and I on the other.

I pushed myself to my feet. "Maybe I am tired," I said. "I'll go in and nap for a little while."

I heard Michael's limping stride retreat down the balcony. Although I lay down and buried my face in the pillows, I couldn't sleep.

The next morning Michael told us that he and Annetta were going to Austin for three days.

"Take Robin's stones," Henley said. "Sebastian asked me to remind you. She wants earrings made of them."

"It's not necessary," I protested.

"But it is," Annetta cried. "Why, I think that's a gorgeous idea. Then you'll have some like mine. Emeralds to emphasize your auburn hair and your green eyes. Michael, make her give them to you."

Michael looked puzzled. "Don't you want earrings, Robin?"

Jamie cut in. "She's the difficult type. She doesn't know what she wants."

"I'll get them," I said and fled upstairs.

The stones were still in the drawer, wrapped in the handkerchief, where I'd put them.

I brought them down to Michael. He stuffed the handkerchief into his shirt pocket. "Okay. We'll see you in three days. Ready, Annetta?"

"Ready?" she cried. "Michael, I've already flown halfway there on my own wings."

They went out together, laughing. The house suddenly seemed extremely quiet. Henley excused himself and went in to see Sebastian. Jamie mumbled something—I didn't know what—and got into the convertible. He drove away in a scattering of gravel. I knew he'd gone into town, to the cafe, to drink beer and kill several hours.

When Jamie came back, I told him he was making a mistake. "You won't change Sebastian's mind by swilling beer."

He gave me a twisted grin. "Do you think that's what I've really been doing?"

"How do I know?"

"Maybe I've got a girl in town."

I shrugged indifferently.

"What do you think I am, Robin. A saint?"

"I know you're not a saint," I said hotly. "And, as for the rest, don't tell me about it. It's no business of mine. I just want to get what we came for and to get out of here."

"Why, Robin, little Robin, are you jealous?" Jamie's hands curled around my cheeks, tipped my face up.

"We had a business arrangement," I said bluntly, pulling away.

"Still, if I hadn't found me a girl in town, I might be giving you a hard time."

"That's rotten," I cried. "Do me a favor. Don't let me see that side of you, Jamie."

"Calm down." He laughed. "I was teasing you."

But I knew he hadn't been teasing me at all. He had allowed himself to show me another facet of his ruthlessness.

The three days dragged miserably without Michael and Annetta there. Jamie spent most of his time in town. When I tried to tell him that he was ruining his chance with Sebastian, Jamie was offhand. "Suppose you leave the rest to me since you've done your part of the job."

I spent hours with Sebastian, slept a lot in the afternoons, looked at the changing colors of the valley below us. But always I sensed the ominous waiting stillness of the house. With dread ever-present in me, it was hard to respond to Annetta's extravagant joy, when she returned with Michael.

It had been an odd breathless day, not a mountain day at all, Sebastian had told me a number of times. A huge rack of thunderheads scudded across the horizon, fuzzy white but shot through with ribbons of black. The air was thick, and stuck in my throat. Jamie had not put in an appearance since early morning.

Annetta came dancing in ahead of Michael, shouting, "We're home, everybody! Look at me! We're home!" And, bursting with excitement, "You'll never guess, Robin. Michael actually took me to Dallas, to Neiman-Marcus. So look at me, will you?"

She was wearing a green linen suit, black patent leather high heels. She was slim and lovely and coltish as always, her bright jet eyes glowing. "We went to Neiman-Marcus, and it was because of you, Robin! He wanted to get your earrings fixed for you. Give them to Robin," she cried. "Hurry up, Michael, let's see if she likes what I chose."

So there, in the main hall, Michael gravely offered me a small golden box, while Annetta danced into the study, crying, "Sebastian, look at me!"

I snapped the box open, and gasped at the two emeralds that sparkled up at me from a bed of white satin. They had been threaded with inch-long golden chains.

"Try them on," Michael said.

I tightened the gold clips at my ears.

From the doorway, Annetta cried, "Perfect. What did I tell you, Michael?" She went on to me, "The fuss he made. You'd think he was trying to please a fractious queen, at least. Anybody'd like them. You do, don't you?"

"Of course," I told her, and glanced at Michael. I saw faint pleasure touch his gray eyes before he limped into the study to talk to Sebastian.

I had the odd feeling, then, that Michael, not Sebastian, had given me the gift. The thought made me feel absurdly pleased. Worse, I was absurdly pleased to have him home again.

I was relieved when it was eventually late enough for

me to pretend to be tired and to go up to bed, leaving Michael and Annetta with Sebastian.

It had been a difficult afternoon and evening. The combination of hot, breathless air and slowly accumulating tension had teased all my nerves to a humming pitch. Jamie had not shown up. Sebastian had given me more than one questioning, then sympathizing glance. And, too often, I had found Michael watching me.

I undressed, turned the lights off, listening to the slow distant rumble of thunder. I curled up in bed, but I couldn't sleep. I kept asking myself what would happen. I kept asking myself how long I could go on with this deception.

Soon I heard Michael and Annetta in the hallway, and, later, the sounds of the house settling down for the night. Thunder rumbled closer and closer. The drapes billowed and danced on a sudden wind. I got up to close the windows as hail the size of golf balls suddenly came pounding in from the dark. The room brightened as great streaks of forked lightning split the sky, and shook as thunder crackled and rolled and echoed from the walls.

Frightened without knowing why, I paced the floor in the dark, and wished that I weren't alone. My mind was full of a burning dread that lashed me as the storm lashed the house.

With a terrible noise, the big windows burst inward. The drapes reached for me. A gusty wind spun through the dark room. I didn't know what had happened. I didn't care. It was as if a giant hand were at my back, thrusting me forward.

I ran into the hall. I wanted to go to Sebastian, to tell him the truth. I wanted him to know I was deceiving him. That I wasn't truly Jamie's wife; that I never would be. I wanted Sebastian to tell me that he forgave me before I left Cromwell Crossing forever.

I ran through the dark, the sounds of thunder pursuing me, like witnesses to my awful guilt. I brushed the damask hanging that covered the door to the recreation room upstairs. It moved under my fingers as I stumbled into the dark oval of the stairs and plunged down.

Then, when it was too late, I knew that I had been led to that moment. My feet caught, clung, I was suspended in mid-air, halfway between falling forward, halfway between fighting to get my balance before I tumbled down the steep flight to the floor below.

Chapter *THIRTEEN*

IN SECONDS swimming the air with frantic flailing arms, I died and died again. A soundless scream choked my throat. My hooked ankles kicked. My body arched away from the sinking darkness below.

Then, caught, snatched back, I fought as a drowning man will, not recognizing rescue when it is offered, but terror-driven to cling and hold to something. I struggled and scratched in a bitter stillness, broken only by my own raw gasps, until familiar arms encircled me, growing tighter, and a familiar voice, not toneless this time, said, "Robin, Robin, it's all right now."

I went limp; my body melted.

Momentarily, my terror was gone with my strength. In that vulnerability induced by a brush of death's wings, I knew love for the first time. I knew it, recognized it, and put it quickly away from me.

"Michael!" I cried. "Oh, Michael——"

"Be still," he whispered. "Be still, Robin."

I found myself magically back in the suite, a trembling huddle on the sofa.

The lights were on now. Michael was at the bedroom door, looking, I realized, at the blowing drapes. He went in. I heard him close and latch the double doors of the window. Instantly the wild wind, the storm itself, receded.

Michael returned with a blanket. He tucked it around me.

I cringed away from his touch, unable to look at him, afraid he would see my heart in my eyes.

"What were you doing out there?" he demanded.

"I was going to——"

I stopped myself just in time, remembering the guilt that had driven me to the dark stairs, the guilt and the bursting windows and the invading storm. My terror came flooding back.

My voice shook as I told him, "I wanted to get something to read."

"What a wildcat!" he said, smiling faintly. "I thought you'd scratch my eyes out before I got a good grip on you."

"I tripped, Michael. It's happened again. It wasn't an accident. There was something that——"

His faint smile died. "Wait," he said brusquely, and disappeared into the hallway.

I sat there, shivering, holding the blanket in tight fingers as a baby grasps his pacifier.

Michael came back, his face a stony mask. "You're mistaken, Robin. If you tripped, it was over your own feet."

I bent my head, remembering the tangle and tug at my ankles as I went racing down in the dark. Sickness flooded through me, the dark rising up to capture me again.

"There was something across the steps, Michael."

"See for yourself, Robin."

He followed me out, touched a switch. Pink light and pale shadows bathed the hallway.

I looked carefully down the steep stairs. I couldn't see anything. I started down.

Michael said, "Don't be foolish, Robin."

But I kept going. At the third or fourth step, I paused to look at the banister rungs. A small thin line, white against the dark of the polished mahogany caught my eye. "Here," I said triumphantly.

"But there's nothing there now. That's probably an old scratch."

I went up the stairs slowly, swallowing against the sudden clutch of tears in my throat.

"You knew, Michael. You took it away."

"I?"

"Of course. No one else was here. You have it in your pocket, don't you?"

He put a hand on my shoulder, turned me, pressed me ahead of him into my suite. I went before him like a convict to the gallows, convinced that soon the noose would be around my neck, yet unable to believe that the trap would truly open.

But, in my room, Michael said, "Robin, you were right, of course." His face was drawn, bleak. "There was a wire stretched across the steps, looped from the rung to a carpet tack in the baseboard." He withdrew his right hand from his pocket. A thin silver-looking strand glinted at me. "But I want you to forget it, Robin," he went on grimly. "We can't tell Sebastian about this."

I took a long slow breath. "We don't have to tell Sebastian. But what can I do? Why does someone here hate me so, Michael?"

"You can leave Cromwell Crossing," Michael said slowly. He went out, closing the door behind him.

Alone, I looked around the silent room. The lamp

glowed on the green carpet, the polished wood furniture. There were no answers here. I dragged myself up, went into the bedroom.

The storm had passed over, but rain whispered at the wide double doors of the window. I checked and re-checked the latch, and, at last, lay down on the bed.

I went over the list of everyone in the house. Who could hate me so much? Why? Who would gain from my absence or death? I dismissed Henley and Maria. I dismissed Sebastian. Annetta was a sweet, but undisciplined, child. Jamie had brought me here. And Michael——— but why would it be he?

Or was there simply no reason? Was there a madman walking the dark halls of Cromwell Crossing? I knew I had somehow missed the truth. For someone in the sad old house was determined to destroy me.

I waited interminable hours for Jamie to come home. By the time he did, my shivering body had finally stilled. I told him what had happened.

"But you didn't fall." He grinned, as usual. "Now that was a lucky break, wasn't it?"

"There was no luck involved," I said soberly. "If Michael hadn't heard me go out, been there to grab me———"

"Michael again?" Jamie asked thoughtfully.

"Will you listen? It couldn't have been an accident, Jamie. It's all part of the same thing. The jardiniere pushed at me, and———"

"Robin, are you losing your mind, or something?" Jamie laughed. "What if a planter fell? A simple accident, nothing more. And how could you get lost in the caves when Michael and Annetta were right there? You just panicked and ran. Like you did tonight. As for the wire———" he went on thoughtfully, "that's probably poor Maria up to one of her Indian tricks. Surely, you know she doesn't mean you harm?" He grinned broadly. "It was most likely a fertility rite."

The smile faded off his face. Jamie's pale-blue eyes regarded me suspiciously. "I suppose you're now going to inform me that you're all through. You want to cut and run as far as you can go. Scruples have blossomed in your heart. I wonder why, Robin. Where did the scruples come from so miraculously?"

I shook my head wearily. "I didn't say anything about giving up, Jamie." But, momentarily, I thought of my small city room. I wished I were back there, mending the worn chair, setting the alarm clock so I wouldn't be late for work to model clothes I knew I would never be able to own.

Then the familiar alluring bright images of wealth filtered past my mind's eye. I told myself to hang on just a little longer. Only a weakkneed coward would cut and run from danger. If I had courage enough to come to Cromwell Crossing, then I must have courage enough to stay. And soon, surely, Sebastian must see—but *what* must Sebastian see? That Jamie deserved a settlement? The more I grew to know the various faces my pseudo-husband wore, the less I believed that to be true. But it didn't matter. We were here to get what we wanted, not what we deserved.

"I don't plan on running away," I told Jamie in a steady voice. "I do think you should speed up the action if you can though."

"Scared, Robin?"

I made myself laugh. "Sure I'm scared. But not scared enough to be driven away."

Jamie's sometime sensitivity must have failed him then. He seemed to accept my show of bravado at face value. He didn't seem to guess that my heart had started to pound with sudden fright at the challenge in my words.

My auburn hair and green eyes stood me in good stead once more as a cover-up.

"Good girl," Jamie drawled. "I didn't really think you'd want to quit. Not now. that you know how much you have to gain."

In the morning, the storm-washed sky was blue and peaceful. The valley lay dreaming in the sun. I lingered on the balcony, wishing I never had to go downstairs to face the Cromwells.

I could present a false face to them, but I could no longer pretend any courage to myself; I couldn't even pretend I had any pride.

But, when I read to Sebastian that morning, listened to his slow voice reminisce about history, I forgot how I felt. His deep-blue eyes seemed more tired than ever, the mauve patches below them even deeper. He paused between words, waiting for each precious breath to come to him.

Sebastian stopped me in the middle of a sentence. "Robin, are you happy here? You have enough to do? Is there anything you want?"

"Everything's fine," I assured him.

"I don't know," the old man went on uneasily. "You're so young, you and Jamie, and this house——"

"Why, Sebastian, what are you talking about?"

He gave me a grin. "I don't know myself, girl." Then, suddenly, he demanded, "Why don't you wear those emerald earrings? Don't you like them?"

"Of course, I do."

"Only—but—then why?"

"They're so fine. I'm afraid I'll lose them, Sebastian."

"And if you do?" Sebastian's grin was vital and alive. "Why, girl, if you do, you'll have replacements to wear."

"You shouldn't be so generous," I protested. "You'll spoil me."

"Why not?" The invalid paused, then went on tiredly. "I think it would be hard to spoil you. I don't understand it, girl. I want to do the right thing. But Jamie's pacing like a lion on a leash. You think I don't know it? And Michael—he's turned so far in on himself I feel he might pop if you poked him. Then there's Annetta, refusing to grow up. I've done her harm, not meaning to, by letting her stay home with me too steadily and too long."

"She loves you, Sebastian—you and the boys."

"Too much," Sebastian said. "That's why she won't grow up. But we'll all go away from her one day. It has to be like that." He sighed, leaned his head back. "Girl, how did you manage to become what you are? How did you manage it all alone and on your own? How come you're decent, and hard-working, and know how to take care of yourself?"

My throat closed up. A blush of shame burned my cheeks. I looked down at the floor, certain he could read my guilt in my eyes.

"Decent, hard-working. Me?"

Poor Sebastian——

I think I might have confessed my guilt right then except that I knew how much it would hurt Sebastian to know that I had come to Cromwell Crossing to help Jamie in a con game. I knew how much it would hurt this kind man because he trusted me, had given his heart to me, just as I had given my heart to him.

Once again, I wondered if I loved him because he was the father I had always wanted, but I realized that reasons didn't matter. It was enough to know that I did love him, had to protect him.

"Well, go on, girl. Read to me some more," Sebastian was saying. "I don't really expect you to explain the deep dark mysteries of life to me."

I made a small smile for him then and, fighting to

keep my voice steady, I read on, losing myself in the words.

At lunchtime, Annetta came in, following Henley with Sebastian's tray. Sebastian suggested that I have lunch with him, but I demurred and made my escape. I passed the door of Michael's room, and saw him standing at the window, looking out at the slope of the red mountain behind the house.

A moment later, Annetta shouted outside my suite. I called to her, and she came in. "We're going to town. Jamie and me. Want to come?" she invited.

"I guess not," I told her.

"Don't you hate reading that stuff to Sebastian? I think you're sweet to do it."

"I like it, Annetta."

"Like it?" Annetta groaned. "Oh, all that old stuff— honestly——"

"That's history, Annetta."

"But who cares?"

"It's interesting."

A momentary blankness touched Annetta's face. "Not to me. Not to Jamie. Just to you and Michael and Sebastian."

I had the weird feeling that she was drawing up some kind of battlelines.

I said gently, "Oh, one of these days you and Jamie will understand how Sebastian feels."

"I don't have to. I just love him. That's all that matters."

I remembered that only a little while before I had thought that, too. Now, I saw that love wasn't enough. Real love had understanding, care, woven into it. Unaccountably Michael came to my mind.

But Annetta didn't wait for my answer. She went down to meet Jamie at the car.

Michael appeared at the door she had left open. "All right, Robin?"

I nodded, though seeing him again had started the slow boil of terror in me. Once more, I felt as if I were falling through the dark in free space, fighting empty air to regain my balance.

Michael hesitated before he said, "But you will be careful, won't you?"

I whispered harshly, "I don't know what to be careful of, Michael."

Chapter *FOURTEEN*

THAT NIGHT I realized that Jamie had taken to heart my suggestion that he speed things up, and I wished that I hadn't said a word. It was after dinner. We were in the huge pink-lighted living room, having brandy. Sebastian, breaking his usual routine, had stayed with us. He sat in a big chair; Annetta was on the floor, leaning against his long legs.

I had worn a dark-green dress that left my arms and shoulders bare and emphasized the narrowness of my waist. At the last minute, following Jamie's suggestion, I clipped on the emerald earrings.

"It'll make old Sebastian feel good to see you wearing them," Jamie had said then.

When I saw how he had set the stage, I understood why he had considered that along with everything else. Jamie had been playing at being the much-in-love husband all through dinner. It reached the point where I began to think I would have to get up and leave, I was so embarrassed by his attentions.

Afterwards, in the living room, he waited until I sat on the sofa, then plunked himself down, leaning back, and holding my hand. He even picked his moment carefully.

When Michael had finished his drink, he got up, saying, "I'll go in to see the Robards' for a while."

Sebastian suggested the rest of us might want to go along.

But Jamie grinned amiably. "No, I guess not, Sebastian. I like it here."

Michael, at the door, turned back, his face suddenly watchful. I wished I weren't always so conscious of him. I wished I hadn't thought of him as I had hooked the belt snugly around my waist, and looked at the revealing dip of the neckline of my dress.

Sebastian said in his slow way, "That's the nicest thing I've heard in a long time."

"Sure, you know I like it here, Sebastian. It's home."

"Home——" Sebastian said.

Annetta moved in a restless sprawl of long slim legs. The diamond earrings sparkled as she swung her hair back. Jamie's fingers stroked my arm. I was overly aware of Michael's eyes, looking at us, of that pale speculative, measuring stare that studied Jamie and me as if we were butterflies impaled on pins.

"Only we can't stay here forever, can we? You know the answer, Sebastian." Jamie leaned forward, his boyish grin frank, open, honest. "I never wanted to ask you, Sebastian. I thought sure you'd see it yourself and go ahead and do it. But it looks like you're so taken with my wife, with Robin, that you're trying to pretend you've forgotten all about it. I guess that's a compliment in a way—your wanting us to stay on here so much that you'd try to keep us here no matter what."

Sebastian raised his gray head; his dark-blue surprisingly sharp eyes seemed to stab at Jamie. "What do you think you're getting at, boy?"

"The settlement, Sebastian. A settlement like you gave to Michael. I'm married now, and I'm ready for one, too."

"You're not ready until you show you're a Cromwell all the way, Jamie."

"Then I guess Robin and I might as well leave," Jamie said calmly.

"Why, you'll do what you want," Sebastian told him. "Only remember, you'll be on an allowance until you act like a grownup, no matter what you say or do. You'll be on an allowance until I die, and, maybe, after as well."

Jamie grinned, but there was an ugly look in his eyes. "Are you threatening me, Sebastian?"

I had a sudden recollection of how Jamie had looked when he was going through that mock courtship with me, sitting across the table, his face bright in the candlelight, his eyes aglow. I wondered if, when he left Cromwell Crossing, his eyes would be shining again.

"I'm telling you," Sebastian was saying. He pushed himself to his feet, looked at me. "Girl, tell me, really, am I a mean unreasonable old man to want my boy to prove himself?"

I didn't know what to say. Jamie's fingers had tightened painfully around my hand.

Finally, I whispered, "You have the right to decide, Sebastian."

Sebastian nodded. "And I have decided."

Later, when we were alone, I told Jamie he shouldn't have done that to Sebastian.

"Why not?"

I hesitated. Then, "You won't change his mind by threatening to go away with me. He doesn't care all that much about me, and, after all, why should he?"

"Why he should I don't know. But he does, Robin, and he doesn't want to let you go." Jamie grinned impishly. "Maybe it's the idea of a long line of grandchildren about to pop out."

I ignored that. "He won't give in, Jamie."

Jamie gave me a mischievous look. "I've given him due warning anyhow. Whatever happens now is on his head."

"What does that mean?"

"I'm going to get what I came for," Jamie said.

"Then why don't you work for him, do whatever he wants? As soon as he thinks you've accepted his conditions, you can have the money, and then you can do what you want."

"Now isn't that your sweet little con girl head working right for a change?" Jamie looked pleased. "Except for one thing. Sebastian's too smart. He'd have some strings on any money for too long, and, if I pulled anything, he'd blow the whistle on me."

"Wouldn't he do the same if he thought we were getting a divorce?"

"You don't give his old man's heart enough credit, Robin. He'd never want to hurt you. If we divorced, he'd assume I was a rotten husband as well as a rotten son, but he'd never cut you off, so he couldn't cut me off either. Get it?"

"Not very well."

"Then don't try."

"But what are you going to do?"

"Let me worry about that." Jamie got to his feet. He touched my earrings, set the bright emeralds dancing. "I can figure something out."

"Jamie, be careful. Sebastian's a sick man, an old man. You might be sorry one of these days."

"Your concern for old Sebastian touches me," Jamie said ironically.

I felt choked, stifled. I needed air. I went down to the main hall, then out the valley door; I sat on the stone steps of the porch.

I looked down at the dark terrace, the few twinkling lights from town, and wondered how much longer I could force myself to stay in Cromwell Crossing, hating myself, and afraid at the same time.

There were quick irregular footsteps against the terrace flags. A tall shadow moved through the dark and became Michael; his face was a blur as he stood at the bottom of the steps.

"I thought you were going to be careful," he said.

I laughed bitterly. "After all, there were so many accidents, Michael. How can one prevent accidents?"

He came up swiftly, took my arms. "Robin, don't go flippant now."

"What else can I be?" I demanded.

He didn't answer me.

I tried to step back, but Michael held me.

We stood there, in the dark of the porch, frozen, staring at each other. Both of us, I knew it was both of us, melting toward each other, yet not allowing ourselves to embrace.

Jamie sneered from the front door, "Has the moral Michael fallen at last? Or is this to be a matter of 'turn about is fair play?' Regardless, I'll thank you to keep your hands off my wife."

"Jamie!" I gasped.

"So this is why you've grown so fainthearted, Robin. You have other irons in the fire now?"

"What are you talking about?" I demanded.

But Michael cut in, said evenly, "Shut up, Jamie, you needn't insult Robin."

"But what am I to think?" Jamie retorted.

"Whatever you want," I cried, and ran inside.

Later, when Jamie came upstairs, his face red with brandy, he asked, "You think all the Cromwells are saints but me, don't you?"

"You certainly aren't."

"Now honey—"

"And don't call me 'honey.' "

"All right. Only maybe you ought to know that the sainted Michael's sainted wife Ayren wasn't so much of a saint after all, and Michael knew it, too."

"Stop hinting and say what you mean," I cried.

"Family secrets, honey—oh, yes, I mustn't call you 'honey'—family secrets. Nobody knows but me, and Michael. And, of course, Ayren knew—but she's dead."

"Jamie, you're being ugly." Now I wished I hadn't told him to say what he meant, but it was too late to stop him.

"Oh, I know, one oughtn't to be honest enough to speak ill of the dead. On the other hand, what's to be done if there's no good to speak of them?"

"Then you can keep quiet."

"Aren't you the least bit curious?"

"No."

"Of course, you are. You're burning to know what I'm talking about. Poor Michael, he married him a live one. Ayren, my, that was a woman for you, an all-around type. She had to have a hand in everything. And *on* everything. A real manager, her. Took over the house, she did, took over Michael, and Sebastian, and Annetta—poor little thing—never knew what hit her. Then Ayren went to work on me. That wasn't so easy."

"I can imagine."

"But she worked it. She tried the brother bit, only what did I need a sister for? So she tried——"

"All right," I cut in, feeling sick, "that's enough, Jamie. You don't need to draw pictures."

"So when I saw Michael hanging onto you for dear life—"

"You don't think he'd ever behave the way you behave!" I flared.

Jamie's eyes narrowed. "You act as if maybe he already has."

I went into the bedroom and slammed the door between us.

But I heard Jamie say, "All right, Robin, only you can't blame a man for wondering, can you? Not when he tags you like a cat after catnip."

I put my hands over my ears. I didn't want to listen any more. I couldn't answer him.

Chapter *FIFTEEN*

I WAS ON the balcony, looking at the faint fading line of the distant horizon. The morning sun warmed my chilled hands. The blue haze in the valley eased my burning eyes. Soon the evil dreams of the night began to fade—Jamie's voice, and Michael's face, and even the waiting silence of the house behind me. The high country, Sebastian's high country, once again worked its magic. I wondered how it was that I could feel as if I had come home, come home to this strange place, when, at Cromwell's Crossing, I had been taught the meaning of terror. It was as if there were two Robins: one who walked in fear, and the other who loved and watched, not believing the menace was real.

The balustrade cast black shadows at my feet, so it was time to go down. I decided to go around the balcony to the outside staircase.

In the breathless stillness that surrounded the house, the voices came at me suddenly, so suddenly that I didn't have time to give warning of my approach. I didn't mean to eavesdrop, but after the first few words, I was rooted there—listening and unable to move.

"The diamonds?" Annetta taunted. "You want to know about the Galveston diamonds? Hah!"

And Jamie: "I'll bet you don't know yourself."

"What I don't know about this house, you could squeeze under this thumbnail."

"Braggart! You're just talking to hear yourself."

A wise little giggle, then: "You don't get me that way, Jamie."

A complimentary laugh. "Okay, Annetta. Then how?"

"Hah! Why should I tell you?"

"You're a big talker." Jamie laughed. "Why don't you put your proof where your mouth is?"

"Why should I?"

"I'll bet I can guess where Sebastian keeps them."

Annetta laughed again. "Then guess, brother."

"You want to play games?"

"I don't have to. I know where they are."

"And I can find them myself, without your help."

"Can you?" Annetta's voice was shrill. "Then go ahead. Do it."

Jamie became sweet, wistful. "You don't sound like yourself any more, Annetta."

"If you hadn't gone away and left me for so long, maybe it would have been different."

"What does that mean?"

"It means," she crowed, "that you'd know where the diamonds are, too." She went on, between giggles, and I could imagine her flinging back her dark curls, giving Jamie a bright malicious look out of her sparkling eyes. "You didn't even *know* about the Galveston deal. I did. I've known for five years."

"Fat chance! Old Sebastian doesn't tell a soul anything. Who are you kidding?"

"He never *told* me. You can be sure of that. I just knew. I saw them, and I saw him handling them. But I was smart. When he gave me the stones for my birthday last year, I acted so surprised, I even felt surprised." Annetta giggled again. "Oh, that was funny!"

Jamie laughed with her. "I can see how it was. Nobody knew but you. You had everybody fooled."

"You're still trying to get around me," Annetta said. "Do you really think I'm going to tell *you* where those stones are stashed?"

"I still can't see why not." Jamie drawled.

"Because I love you," she said sweetly. "And once you get your hands on them, you'll go away." And then in a sullen tone, "Besides, you're not the only one who wants to know."

I was rooted there, my hands clenched into fists, my throat tight against a deep rising sickness that I could barely control.

A golden drape billowed from the window of Annetta's room, which Jamie, mockingly, had called the nursery— A nursery where evil children played a grotesque game.

I stumbled forward, fled around the corner of the house, and froze at the top of the steps.

Michael, head bent, his face in shadow, was coming up. He heard me, and straightened up. For an endless moment, we stared at each other. I didn't know if he'd heard Annetta and Jamie talking. I didn't dare ask. He looked at me with the same expressionless look that always managed to frighten me, but he didn't make a sound.

I turned and fled to the safety of my bedroom, trying to think, wondering if I could persuade Jamie to give up his awful plan.

Now I knew what he'd meant when he told me that he was giving Sebastian a last chance. "Due warning," Jamie had called it, adding that he would figure something out since it seemed he wouldn't ever get the settlement he wanted.

He intended to steal the Galveston stones. To steal them from his own father!

I knew. Oh, I knew how he would work it. He would tease and taunt Annetta until he got the location of Sebastian's hiding place from her. He would play on her, promise her anything, to get what he wanted. And poor Annetta—in the end, she would have to give in. Because all she really wanted was Jamie's love.

I couldn't bear my thoughts.

I went into the hall. Michael's door was open, but the room was empty. The desk was piled high with papers. The reflecting sunlight off the mountain slope beyond the window spilled a trail of pink on the beige carpet.

I glanced down the passageway. Annetta's door was closed. They were still there, matching wits. But I knew who would win. Jamie, ruthless and without feeling, knowing Annetta inside and out, would have his way, if not at the moment, then sometime soon.

I wondered if Michael had heard, if he knew and understood. I wondered what he could do to keep Sebastian from being hurt once again. I went down the wide staircase. Automatically, my eyes sought out the thin white scar on one of the banister rungs. My footsteps were silent on the rug.

Henley was standing in the main hall.

He visibly twitched when I asked if Sebastian were resting. I wondered what was wrong. But Henley said I could go in if I wanted to.

I said hastily, "No, I won't disturb him," and went into the living room, knowing that he was watching me. I turned back to look. He was—his glasses twinkling. He gave me a small tight smile.

My feet were silent on the Oriental rugs. I glanced at the mahogany tables, the huge framed paintings, the velvet drapes, the ceramic pots shining in the dimness—like candles of hope in a church. Beautiful beautiful things, I thought. I stopped abruptly. But what good were beautiful things when a heart was full of hate instead of love, when evil pulled the strings and puppets danced?

I shivered and pushed open the door to the kitchen. Maria turned, a warm loving smile on her face—the smile that told me she knew it would be me before she actually saw me—the smile that always shamed me because I didn't deserve it. The same welcoming smile faltered slowly, and faded, and her round dusky face became troubled, her ageless eyes looking deep into me.

"What is it, Robin?" She gestured at the table. She moved a few small things, then came, soundless on her small boots, to sit opposite me. "What is it, Robin?" she asked somberly.

I shook my head. I looked at the closed door beyond her shoulder. The closed door to the room which was her home—a pine-scented, picture-filled refuge from the secrets of Cromwell Crossing. I wished I could hide in there forever.

"You are worried," Maria said softly. "You are frightened in your soul."

I didn't answer, but raised my eyes to meet her probing look.

Her face was touched with a sudden deep terror. It

put lines into her cheeks, fire into her black slanted eyes.

"Robin?"

"Do you ever make magic?" I asked softly, thinking of the thin wire strung across the dark stairs, the clutch and pull of it on my ankles. "Do you, Maria?"

"I? No. I do not make magic." She sighed. "If I did, I would long ago have cured this house." Suddenly, all terror was wiped from her face. She was half smiling, "But why?"

"There are things," I said vaguely.

"What things, Robin?"

"I don't know—I don't know what to do——"

She pushed herself up. "All will be well, Robin. I know. I know."

"But Jamie——"

She waited.

I had stopped, and then found that I couldn't go on. I daren't tell her what Jamie planned. I had to stop him myself. It was my job, and mine alone. Expiation for the false wedding band I wore.

I got up and said, "Maybe it's all a dream." I tried to smile.

Maria agreed solemnly, the foreign rhythm in her speech making an incantation of her words. "Yes, Robin, it is all a dream. But it will end well. It will end well."

Sensing her assurance, trying to understand it, I went out to the terrace. For a little while, I studied the wide panorama below. Then something made me turn. Henley was on the porch.

I glanced upward. I saw Jamie angling along the balcony, hands in his pockets, shoulders slumped. Beyond him, the long wide windows caught the sun, reflecting a dozen glittering eyes, a dozen demon eyes.

I remembered how, when I had first seen Cromwell Crossing from the valley, I had been afraid. Now, full of dread, and with good cause, I went into the house.

I found Jamie in our suite, pacing the floor, mumbling words under his breath. I closed the door behind me, leaned against the firm thick panel for strength.

"Jamie, you can't do it."

He glanced at me, his pale-blue eyes narrowed.

"Jamie, listen, I heard you working on Annetta. It wasn't hard to figure out what you were up to."

"Okay, so you snooped, and you've got it all figured out. So what?"

"But you just can't do it, Jamie. You'll break Sebastian's heart."

"Not him. His heart doesn't break. He's a Cromwell."

"Jamie, if you'd only have patience."

"I'll have enough patience." He grinned at me, a thin narrow twist of the lips. "Enough to work on Annetta until I find out. You can be sure of that."

"But you can't steal from your own father, Jamie."

"Why not?" Jamie grinned. "Sebastian's got no more right to those stones than I have. So I'm going to get them before somebody else does."

I understood then the meaning of a father's sins being visited on the sons. I knew I couldn't make Jamie see that it was wrong to steal, even to steal stolen goods. He was proud to be living out the old buccaneer streak that Sebastian had spoken of.

"I may not be the only one who wants those diamonds, but I'm going to get there first. Just watch me make the beginning of a new Cromwell fortune. The Jamie Cromwell fortune."

"It would be best to forget it, Jamie. To give up, on the settlement, on the diamonds, to go away. Now, Jamie. Now."

"Scruples, Robin? All of a sudden you have scruples."

"Please, Jamie."

"Don't worry. You'll get your share of the diamonds. I'm not planning to cut you out."

"I don't want anything, Jamie. I won't take anything."

He stared at me. "Double for me if that's the case." Then, "You really do have scruples. My, my, honey, isn't it late for that line?"

"Not too late. Not yet." I paused; then went on deliberately, "I mean it, Jamie."

"Oh, grow up."

"I have. Just this morning. I've started to think."

"And what do you think you're going to do?"

I took a long slow breath. "I'm going to do whatever I have to do to stop you. I'll go to Sebastian to tell him the truth. I'll tell him why you brought me home with you, and then I'll pack up and leave."

I knew it would hurt Sebastian to have me go, hurt him to know my deception. Yet, I was terribly afraid that Jamie would hurt Sebastian even more if we stayed on. I took another long slow breath. "I promise you, Jamie. I won't sit still while you——"

He laughed at me. "Robin, don't you know? Haven't you guessed? With the diamonds waiting for me, I don't need you——"

"But——"

"Yes. But——" He came close to me. "I don't care what you do. Except for one thing." His fingers closed around my shoulders, bit deep. "If you say a word before I've got my hands on that sackful of sweet future, I'll pitch you over the terrace. I'll shove you over into the treetops, and you'll catch and hook and tear all the way to the bottom, leaving bits of your body trailing behind, streamers of Robin shredded on the sharp spruce like red tinsel on a Christmas tree." He shook me lightly. The razor rasp went out of his voice. He said, "You had better believe me."

Annetta called from outside the door. "Jamie, how about it? Want to go to town?"

Jamie grinned at me, suddenly boyish again. "Sure, Annetta. I'll be right there."

He gave me a last touch, fingers stroking my cheek, whispered, "If you're a good girl, and keep your mouth shut as you damn well better, I'll still give you your share. Think about the goodies that will buy for you."

His hands dropped away. I stepped back from him.

"I wouldn't want anything I got that way," I said. "Not any way so low."

He laughed softly as he went out.

Dazed, knowing we were no longer conspirators, but enemies, I went into the bedroom. There, on the dresser, reflected in the mirror, I saw something odd. I stopped in front of it, stared.

It was a full round potato. A thin silver knife was rammed through it.

The message it offered was clear enough for a child to read. I picked it up in my cold hands, turned it, stroked it, trying to exorcise the evil from it. I was still holding it when Maria tapped at the door, came in at my call.

Maria saw the potato, the silver knife thrust into it. She took it from me. "You found this here, Robin?"

I nodded.

Her face was alive with fright, but, after a moment's silence, it cleared. "No more than a child's game. Yes. A child's game."

She smiled at me, a moment of comfort, before she left. Later, she returned, making no excuse, simply looking in, her dark eyes searching the room.

"All alone, Robin?"

"Jamie went driving with Annetta."

Maria nodded, left me again.

I moved restlessly from sofa to bed to chaise unable to find a spot which would offer me a haven. I was driven by my thoughts. I imagined myself taking my suitcase from the closet emptying the drawers, packing before Jamie returned. I imagined myself walking down the road beneath the spruce trees where Ayren had died, walking down the road and leaving, turning my back forever on Cromwell Crossing.

Chapter *SIXTEEN*

I TRIED to remember the crazy impulse that had led me to bring Jamie home with me the night I first saw him. I didn't have the faintest recollection of how I'd felt then. And I couldn't understand why I'd let him talk me into his scheme. The vision of the material things that I'd wanted so much and I didn't have then eluded me.

I thought about the three-times hand-me-down clothes that I'd worn, hating them, as a child. The tiny room I lived in. The feeling of rebellion and fear inside me that I'd grown accustomed to. Was it here, to Cromwell Crossing, that it had led me?

What was the "everything" I'd wanted so much? Where were the bright dreams now?

I looked around the luxurious room. Its furnishings mocked me. They were all *things*. Just *things*. With no value except the value man put upon them. I realized that things didn't matter to me as much as I'd thought. I'd brought Jamie home to my room because I'd been lonely. What I'd missed was love.

I knew I didn't care any more about the money that was to have been my share. I'd given that up as soon as

I heard Jamie talking with Annetta. I'd turned my back on those bright dreams gladly.

I curled deeper into the green chaise. My foot brushed a newspaper Jamie had left there. A black headline told of an old woman murdered in the desert by a hitchhiker she stopped to help. I shuddered and kicked the paper to the floor.

There was a sickness abroad in the world. The same sickness that Jamie had. It made him into a mechanical man, a computing thing, without heart or soul, without the ability to love. And I knew what a contagious disease it was. For I had contracted it, too. Now, in Cromwell Crossing, I realized that I, like Jamie, had harbored the seeds of it in me, and, as in Jamie, those seeds had developed and the fruit was evil.

I wanted to pack, to run away. In spite of Jamie's threat, I was more afraid of staying than going. And yet——

Sebastian? What about Sebastian?

If I left, Jamie wound find some plausible story to tell. Any story but the truth; then he would add to Sebastian's pain by stealing the diamonds as soon as possible, and leaving himself.

And if I didn't leave—my eyes went back to the potato leaning on its silver stake.

Then I buried my face in my hands.

I made up carefully. Light powder under my eyes to hide the dark smudges there. Bright lipstick to make my mouth seem to smile. A dusting of rouge to fill out my hollowed cheeks.

My hands shook at the zipper of my blue skirt. I made tight fists and held my breath, then forced my body to relax. Finally, I tried again. The closing moved easily. I settled a blue overblouse at my hips, and sat down to pull on my nylons. Of the cut on my shin, there was nothing left but a line of almost invisible stitches.

I was stepping into my high-heeled pumps when Jamie knocked, thrust the door open. "Ready?"

I nodded, thinking that I was lucky, at least, that Jamie cared so little for me except as a means to an end —that he had kept to our agreement. I knew now that only lack of interest, not scruples, had prevented him from trying to change our make-believe marriage into something a bit more real. At least, I could be grateful for that.

I went down with Jamie, walking warily, remembering his razor-sharp voice so graphically describing what he would do if I confessed to Sebastian, remembering, too, the silver glint of the knife thrust into that ridiculous potato.

Maria had called it a child's game. But I knew it for what it was. A warning.

Dinner was a silent affair. Sebastian excused himself, retiring early, perhaps responding to the tension in the rest of us.

Annetta told me that she'd seen Uncle Ned Robard, and had been instructed to tell me that we were all to go in to their house for coffee the next morning. "You see," she asked Jamie, "I didn't forget to tell Bobby after all, did I?"

I felt a little ripple of discomfort. Annetta had given up calling me "Bobby" for some time. I wondered why now, suddenly, she had taken it up again.

As usual, Jamie ignored it, but Michael put in, without looking at me, "Annetta, I told you Robin is 'Robin' and nobody else."

Jamie grinned. " 'A rose is a rose is a rose'—so what difference does it make?"

Annetta flung herself out of her chair. "I hate that name," she screamed. "You know I do, Jamie!"

"Sorry," he said. "Really, I just forgot." But his chuckle made the apology meaningless.

The next morning Jamie said, "No, but no thanks. I don't feel like Belinda and Ned today."

Michael shrugged. "Okay, we'll go on then." Before I could demur he said to me, "I'll see you in the car, Robin."

Though I hadn't wanted to be alone with him, I didn't protest. I knew why Jamie had decided to stay behind. He meant to search the house without having the rest of us underfoot.

Annetta was outside, talking with Michael, an arm draped around his shoulder. He put her firmly aside, said gently, "Grow up, Annetta, it's time and time overdue."

Michael had a strange look on his face. A sadness— a fear. . . . He limped around to the driver's seat, and got in. Annetta flung herself in beside him. When I joined them, his face became bleak, impersonal.

After one quick look, I kept my eyes away from him, wishing I didn't have to ride with him. But, ever since Annetta had mentioned the Robards the night before, I had known what I must do.

I couldn't speak to Sebastian. I couldn't speak to anyone in the house. There was only Belinda and Ned to turn to.

I arranged the words carefully in my mind.

Annetta chattered about inconsequentials. Michael grunted an occasional disinterested answer. Once, as I sneaked a quick look at his profile, I saw him slide a glance toward me. I bent my head quickly.

We rolled down the twisting road. I looked ahead, into the curves, wondering if Michael, too, were thinking of Ayren, wondering if he knew the curve where the car had failed, if he knew the exact spot where she had been killed.

At last we reached the stone posts at the gate. I had begun to think of them as guardians of my prison, soldiers deployed before the entrance to Cromwell Crossing.

From the highway, I could look up at the house, and, beyond it, to the mountain that was Rose Cromwell's grave. Michael, too, glanced in that direction. I wondered instantly if he had had the same thought.

The shared knowledge of what lay there in a shadowed alcove had made a bond between us. A bond which I couldn't ignore. But there was more, more. Something drew me to Michael, drew me closer and closer, so that, even in the midst of fear, he was in my thoughts.

In a little while, we were in town.

Annetta cried, "Let's stop at the drugstore."

Michael agreed, drew up in front of the sun-baked adobe building. "Okay. Make it snappy, Annetta. I'll get gas and come back for you."

But, still not wanting to be alone with him, I said I, too, needed some things in the drugstore.

"What?" Annetta demanded.

For a minute, I couldn't think. My mind was a blank. Then I stammered, "Oh, you know, bobby pins, stuff like that."

"Girl stuff," she said, satisfied. "See? It's a good thing I said to stop here. Robin never asks. She's as bashful as when she first came."

"You could stand a shot of that bashfulness," Michael said dryly.

Annetta and I went into the drugstore. She bought a lipstick, while I browsed around, finally picked up a card of bobby pins, and a new powder puff. She decided she wanted a soda, and sat at the fountain. I joined her.

The young blond clerk gave her a bright-eyed look, said, "Hi, Annetta, what's new up on the hill?"

Her face went blank. She stared through him.

He flushed, said coldly, "Okay, what'll you have, miss?"

She told him she wanted a chocolate soda. I ordered the same. He brought them quickly; she gulped hers, then flung herself outside, shouting to me: "Michael's waiting for you."

I had hardly begun to sip my drink, but I put it aside, and paid for both of us.

The young blond clerk grumbled, "She thinks she's the princess of Cromwell Castle, she does. Nobody around town here is good enough for her, nor ever was." He eyed me curiously, went on, "Are you the new one up there? Jamie's wife? Well, you better be careful how you come down that road, and who you come with. All kinds of funny things happen. Cromwell Castle sure is hard on the wives."

I couldn't answer him. My face felt stiff. I took my purse and hurried to the car.

My stunned mind repeated the words over and over again. *"Cromwell Castle sure is hard on the wives."*

I knew from what the clerk had said that in town, at least, Michael was somehow being blamed for Ayren's death. But I knew it could only have been an accident. An accident—there were too many accidents at Cromwell Crossing. Rose, poor Rose, left to moulder in the cave, just as I myself might have; another accident—the planter falling from the balcony; then the tumble down the steps on which the wire could have been placed as quickly as Michael had removed it.

Michael, coming in just as the planter fell.

Michael, suddenly there, following me in the cave.

Michael, on the stairs behind me in the middle of a storm-whipped night.

Michael, on the balcony only minutes before I found the stabbed potato—symbol and warning of a stab for me.

I turned my head. My neck was stiff with fear. Michael? Could he be the one? His face was expressionless, the profile hard and stubborn, the black brows drawn. He turned then, shot me a pale glance that seemed to see into me, see through me.

Could it actually be Michael who hated me so?

It couldn't be Michael. Not when he was the man I could have loved—the man I could have loved if I'd met him in another place, another time. It was as if two deep warring instincts were tearing me apart. I was drawn to him, yet I was afraid of him, too. I felt an involuntary cry of protest on my lips, and bit it back. No, no, it couldn't be Michael!

But who was my enemy? Who?

Annetta's light voice continued to spill words around us as we pulled into the Robards' driveway. I didn't listen. I was too busy arranging my own words in my mind. I had to speak to someone, to ask for help. I was in the dark. Somewhere there must be light. Belinda would know. Belinda would care.

She was at the door to meet us, her gray hair as perfectly waved as always under its gray net, her cheeks pink. She demanded in her high breathless voice, "Where's Jamie?"

When we made excuses for him, she said, "Oh, more's the pity. I made his favorite lemon pie." She waved us in, cried, "Ned? Ned, they're here." She explained, "He's ending office hours in your honor. Can you imagine that?"

The house was cool, lovely. Within its old white-washed walls, I found it hard to believe in the terrors of Cromwell Crossing.

My offer to help Belinda was brushed aside, but Michael and Annetta followed her into the kitchen.

Soon Uncle Ned came in. He gave me a quizzical look

from the doorway, his twisted face turned to one side. "Robin, you are a pale shadow of yourself, you are."

"Thanks for the compliment," I told him, trying to make his concern a joke. "Maybe I forgot my makeup."

"I'm speaking as a doctor, not a gallant." He cocked his head even further. "Don't they feed you right up there?"

"Of course."

"Then what?"

"I'm fine."

"Don't try that gambit. My Belinda has been using it on me for thirty years." Without another word he bounded away. When he came back, he dropped a bottle in my lap. "Take them, one a day. Vitamins. I don't believe in them myself, but for people who won't eat, well, then——"

I wished he wouldn't be nice to me. It made it even harder for me to try to tell Belinda. I felt as if I would spread corruption in this house. When I told Belinda, I would be telling Ned, too. And I must. I knew that I had to speak to someone before—before I lost my mind, before there was another accident—before Jamie found the Galveston diamonds.

Ned said, "I didn't judge you to be nervy when you first came, but now——"

"I'm not, Ned. Not at all."

"They why do you jump at the slightest sound?"

I stared at him.

He went on gently, "Robin, I know, I know, you're not happy. Something is wrong. What are you afraid of?"

I opened my lips. That was the moment. I trusted him. I wanted to tell him, to ask his help.

At that moment, Belinda came bustling in, her full figure arranged in tight curves on her rigid spine. "Now you keep telling me I don't have hot flashes," she said to Ned, "but feel me, touch me, and you'll see." She grinned at me, and for a moment I saw the young girl she must once have been. "Some doctor," she giggled. "Won't believe in my hot flashes." She put a tray on the coffee table, and, straightening, looked from Ned to me and back. "What's the matter?" she demanded.

"Belinda," Ned said in his most professional voice, "I want to talk to Robin for a minute." And then, "Where are Michael and Annetta?"

She flapped her pink hand at him. "Yes, Doctor, I'm going, Doctor, me and my hot flashes. Michael and Annetta are in the patio collecting some hollyhocks to take back to the castle. How long do you want with little Robin?"

"Go on," Ned told her.

She gave me a smile, then sailed out.

Ned turned back to me. "Now, then——"

But the moment was gone. I found that I couldn't tell my awful suspicions to Ned and Belinda. I couldn't contaminate the house they loved with my terrible thoughts and dreadful story.

"Robin?"

"It's nothing," I said stiffly, and looked down at my clenched hands.

He sighed softly. "I don't mean to pry, child. I just had a feeling there was something you wanted to say."

I shook my head.

"If you should ever want to talk about it—to me, to Belinda—remember there's not much we haven't seen. And, sometimes, between a man and his wife—a small thing happens, and it can be put right, but if one waits too long, small things can become big ones, and——"

My cheeks burned. He assumed the problem lay between Jamie and me. Between a husband and his bride.

I choked back a bitter laugh, grateful that Michael and Annetta came in then.

I stole a quick glance at Michael. He was relaxed. A

rare smile lit his face. I realized again how handsome he was. I yearned almost irresistibly to touch his dark hair.

I clenched my hands in my lap, wondering if I were losing my mind. Perhaps the gossip in the town was right. Michael's handsome face, usually so expressionless, might hide murderous thoughts. The accident of Ayren's death could have been no accident at all. After what Jamie had said about Ayren and himself, I could no longer accept Sebastian's picture of Michael's feelings for Ayren. Suppose that, in his vengeful hatred of Jamie, a well-concealed hate, I had to admit, he had decided that I, being Jamie's wife (as he thought) must also die?

"Robin? Robin!"

I heard my name faintly, a call from faraway, a distant echo. I jerked my head up.

Belinda said, "My goodness, child, you're white as a sheet."

"I'm sorry," I said weakly.

"Sorry? For what on earth?" Belinda got up, came to me. "Do you have a fever?" Then, to Ned, "Fine doctor, there you sit, pouring coffee!"

"Leave her be," Ned said. "You pour the coffee and pass the pie. We're all growing tired of waiting."

I gave him a grateful smile as he went on, diverting attention from me, saying, "Some hostess—if she's not complaining about those hot flashes of hers, she's complaining about her husband."

Belinda gave a flustered giggle. "My goodness, I forgot to cut the pie."

Michael laughed softly. I looked up, realizing that it was only here, at the Robards', that I had ever heard that low chuckle. It was as if he were one man here, and another in the house on the mountain. But when I saw his pale eyes, I realized that he was the same man. I knew I was being watched, measured, judged, by his steady glance.

Later, when we were leaving, Ned told me in an undertone to remember that I could always speak to him. He would help me in any way he could. He and Belinda were my friends. I whispered my thanks, and got into the car with Michael and Annetta, grateful, for once, that she was with us.

I didn't know if I could have borne that lonely drive up the mountain alone with Michael, wondering if, somewhere along the way, he would provide another accident for the town to talk about.

I reminded myself that Jamie had said that he and Michael were together when the planter was pushed at me from the balcony. But that didn't help allay my suspicions. I knew Jamie would say anything that suited his purpose, and when he had said that, he hadn't wanted me to think of myself as a possible victim of anyone's evil intent. He hadn't wanted me to become scared enough to leave Cromwell Crossing.

I watched for my first sight of the house, and saw it at last, perched high; in the dark, it sat austerely alone against the sky. Yellow light spilled from the tall windows, unblinking beacons of warning.

The moment's glimpse stiffened me against a quick pinch of fright.

Annetta leaned over and said with satisfaction, "We're almost home."

Chapter *SEVENTEEN*

WE DROVE up behind the house. Michael cut the motor, and silence moved in on us, a silence so profound that the faint whisper of wind in the dark trees sounded like thunder. As we went toward the house, I felt again those waves of melancholy reaching for me. And, once again, I shivered and stopped in my tracks.

"Robin, wait, I want to talk to you," Michael said quietly.

Annetta grabbed his arm. "Oh, talk later. Let's play cards, or listen to records, or do something." She clung to him, like a five-year-old.

I said quickly, "That's a good idea, Annetta."

But Michael said, "Wait, Robin." His voice was so compelling that I found I couldn't move even though I wanted to break into a frantic run.

He put Annetta firmly aside, his face bleak. "Go in," he told her. "We'll be in in a little while."

"But why not now?" Annetta flared. "Robin, Robin, Robin—I can't see why you've always got to talk to her anyhow." She stormed ahead of us, through the black shade of the trees and the brilliance of sun up the steps.

"Tell Sebastian we're back," Michael called after her. But the big door banged open and then slammed shut.

Michael and I stood there, staring at each other, separated by a few feet that might as well have been a chasm.

He said tonelessly, "These kids——"

"I'll go in." I could hear the quaver in my voice. Only, in that moment, listening to Annetta, had I realized the depth of her jealousy of me. She was jealous of *me*—I, who had never been loved, never been wanted. Except, perhaps, by poor deceived Sebastian.

"Please," Michael said. "Please wait, Robin."

It was an order although there was a *please* before it to make it seem polite. Yet that small courtesy only mocked me.

"Cromwell Castle sure is hard on the wives. . . ."

I was afraid, afraid to be alone with Michael even in the hard hot brilliance of the late afternoon sun.

I couldn't hide it. I whispered, "What do you want, Michael?"

"I think you should go away, Robin."

"Go away?" I repeated, unbelieving, for, of course, that was what I wanted, too, wanted more than anything —to escape Cromwell Crossing and the memory of the greed that had brought me there, to escape not only my own guilt, but a danger I couldn't put a name to. Yet I couldn't go. I couldn't, because somehow I had to defeat Jamie's purposes.

Michael took my frightened words, the silence that followed them, as refusal. He said coldly, "You must do as I tell you, Robin."

I burst out, no longer able to control my tongue. "Why do you want to destroy me? Or, failing that, to drive me away?"

He seemed to grow taller, larger, to loom over me, his fingers suddenly tight on my arm. "You little fool. Do you think I'm—are you actually afraid of me? I'm trying to protect you. To protect everyone!"

"To protect me?" I asked bitterly.

He said bleakly, "Yes. Just that. No matter what you think. I believe you should at least go down to

Santa Fé for a while. Tell Sebastian you want to shop. I promise that I'll see that you get there safely."

I thought with longing of the sweet winding streets that I had promised myself to visit again. I thought of the red-tiled roofs and the improbable blue sky that arched over them.

I looked up at Michael. His pale eyes were shadowed by an impenetrable curtain. His mouth was narrowed, grim. I thought of telling him about Jamie, asking if he had heard, if he could avert Jamie.

But I couldn't. Annetta had said that someone else wanted to steal the Galveston jewels. Who could it be but Michael? I accepted that question and the answer to it with a tinge of pain, but I did accept it. I knew that I must stay, must stop Jamie and Michael from hurting Sebastian.

"And if I don't go?" I asked slowly.

He hesitated. Then, "Robin, I don't know what will happen."

"Do you intend that as a threat?"

Michael seemed to draw further into himself, to turn in, his face rock-hard, the shadows making hollows in his cheeks, putting a cruel glitter into his eyes. "Take it however you want," he said tonelessly. "It's up to you now."

He left me standing there. He turned away, quickly became a tall shadow disappearing in the brush as he moved up the slope of the mountain.

I took a slow careful breath and looked up at the silent house, the house that again seemed then like a huge crouching animal—an animal waiting to pounce on some unwary prey.

Inside, in the dimness of the main hall, I paused. I could hear Annetta's light voice, laughing now, underscored by Sebastian's deep slow words.

The Cromwell portraits seemed to sneer at me from their wide golden frames.

I climbed the steps quickly, my eyes shearing away from the thin white line that a tight-strung wire had cut on one of the banister rungs.

It seemed a long way to the upper wing, a long dim way, full of shadows, a rising tunnel. I shuddered, thinking of the passages within the mountain where there lay in an alcove like a church niche an abandoned body in rotting garments, a pair of high-heeled slippers fallen from once-quick feet.

Jamie was in our suite, pacing again.

"Have a ball in town?"

"Belinda made lemon pie for you."

"Lemon pie," Jamie groaned. "Spare me from Belinda's love."

"You do that for yourself."

He scowled. "I had important things to consider."

"You didn't find them." Then, knowing it was useless, I still had to say, "Jamie, give it up. Let's leave."

"I want what's mine, Robin."

"Maybe you won't find the jewels."

He said suddenly, "You don't have to sound so hopeful. You'd think you were on Sebastian's side instead of with me."

"I'm not with you any more."

"With Sebastian——" Jamie sneered. "One word from me——"

"Then give that word."

"If Sebastian knew I'd pulled that kind of a trick——"

"I'll tell him myself, Jamie——"

"No," Jamie said through his teeth. "No, you won't." And with his strange sensitivity about me, "And not because you're scared of what I'll do to you. But you're hooked on Sebastian, aren't you? Hooked on him, and on Michael, too. You don't want to admit how come you're here with me."

"You could be wrong, Jamie."

"I'm not wrong."

And, of course, he wasn't. I couldn't tell Sebastian the truth, nor Michael. In those brief moments when we first met, Jamie had read me well.

"Did you know it would be like this?" I demanded. "Did you, Jamie?"

"Like what?"

"This——" I repeated helplessly, and went on, "the fear, the——"

"There aren't any old ghosts walking through Cromwell Crossing, Robin."

"Only new ones?" I asked.

But he didn't answer me. He went through the bedroom, out of the wide double doors, leaving the curtains blowing behind him. He stood on the balcony, hands braced on the balustrade, his shoulders squared.

I wondered what he saw as he stared toward the twilight haze that blanketed the tiny town in the valley.

I remember that the next few days passed slowly, unreal and drifting. I drifted with them. Yet the house was like a pot of water boiling over a high flame. Tension seethed, steaming through all of us. Only Sebastian seemed aloof, immune, unaware, serene in his conviction that soon Jamie would prove himself to be a true Cromwell, and earn his share of the family fortune.

"You'll see," Sebastian told me once, "Robin, girl, I'm right, and I know it. There's Cromwell in Jamie and it's coming to the fore."

Tears stung my eyes as I turned away. Sebastian was more right than he knew, yet I was certain that the proof he had set his heart on was not that same proof that Jamie intended to give him.

I waited nervously, trying to decide how to make Jamie give up on finding the Galveston jewels.

One morning at breakfast, Annetta, eyeing me over her coffee cup, said, "You're young, Robin, even if you are married—though I must say, you don't seem married to me. You and Jamie——" She gave a peculiarly adult shrug.

Maria said reprovingly, "Annetta, that is not nice," with her odd accent, turned her plump lined face from Annetta to Jamie, then back again without quite looking at me. Seeing her warm glance, I realized what I had wanted all my life, and I knew that I had been searching for something more than material pleasures when I had brought Jamie home with me from the street—when I came to Cromwell Crossing with him. I wondered why I had had to travel so far to learn about love, and to learn about terror, too.

Annetta groaned. "Maria, babying me again! Oh, I'm not ten any more."

"You act like ten, be treated like ten," Maria said, giving Annetta's shoulders a squeeze.

Annetta groaned. "I can't bear it, Robin. Don't you see what I mean? Can't you explain to Maria that I don't need a nursemaid any more?"

I tried to smile. "It's really not as bad as all that, is it, Annetta?"

But I knew what she meant. It seemed to me that I was in the same position that she was. I had become aware gradually that I, too, had scarcely any time to myself. If Maria wasn't with Annetta, then she was with me, smiling somberly, talking of inconsequentials. And there was Henley, always drifting about silently, so much underfoot that I had begun to wonder if he were spying on me.

Michael, more than ever, seemed to make a point of being around. He would join me when I was alone on the balcony. He was silent, withdrawn, stern. But, sometimes, I would catch a glimpse of his pale eyes that set my heart racing before he looked away. And, sometimes, he would tell me stories about when he was a child at Cromwell Crossing, and, then, for long moments, I would forget the waiting stillness of the house, forget my fears, and I would take comfort from being with him.

"It *is* as bad as all that," Annetta was saying, her face glum as a child sent to bed before dark. "Oh, I wonder if I'll ever be happy again."

Maria cried, "Annetta, you must not say such things! You have much to be happy for."

But, once again, I knew how Annetta felt for I, too, wondered if I could ever be happy again.

Then, her eyes suddenly sparkling, Annetta cried, "Robin, tell me all about San Francisco."

"I've never been there," I told her.

"You haven't? But I thought——"

"I met Jamie in Los Angeles."

"But still——"

"I was working, there was never time for a trip, nor money either."

But Annetta had stopped listening. "Some day, I'm going to see San Francisco. North Beach and Russian Hill, and—all of it," she finished triumphantly.

I knew that Jamie had been talking to her, drawing an exciting picture for her of a faraway city. But I knew, too, that he had also been searching the nooks and crannies of the old house. I had seen him, wandering aimlessly, too aimlessly, through all the downstairs rooms, speculatively eyeing the bookcases and copper pots, the tables and drawers, even the fireplaces.

"But there's Sebastian," Annetta was saying. "I couldn't leave him." And then, "Except maybe—just for a little while—for San Francisco——"

She was still in that mood at dinner time. She came

down dressed in a fitted black gown that belled from her knees in ruffles of chiffon. Her black hair was brushed into shining curls that clung to her head. The diamonds sparkled at her ears, dancing as she danced before us.

"Well, now," Sebastian said. "You're a sight for sore eyes."

"My Neiman-Marcus dress," Annetta said proudly. "For when I go to San Francisco, Sebastian." Then, "Michael let me buy it."

But Michael looked grim.

It was Jamie who said, "You're gorgeous. You will be the belle of San Francisco. *If* you ever get there."

Chapter *EIGHTEEN*

I WAS reading to Sebastian. He seemed particularly tired that morning. He lay back on the sofa, silent, not interrupting with stories of the past. The mauve patches under his dark-blue eyes were livid as bruises, and the eyes themselves mirrored far-away thoughts.

Henley sat in the big leather chair, quiet as always. The only movement about him was an occasional flicker as light twinkled from his rimless glasses.

I paused for a moment, and my glance went to the window. It was another of those rare gray days—a thick overcast layered the sky, broken only where a few thicker massed black clouds hung motionless over the valley below. An aura of stillness wrapped the house, a stillness so palpable it seemed to throb. I thought that Cromwell Crossing waited, just as I waited.

I had paused too long.

Sebastian stirred, raised his head. "What's the matter, girl? Are you tired? Want to stop?"

"Oh, no," I told him, and then found a quick excuse for my silence in a patch of yellow on the mountainside. "I just noticed something, Sebastian. The mountain off to the right of us has something I never saw before. A whole area of the hottest yellow color, as if the sun were shining there, but I can't see the sun today."

He chuckled. "The aspens on Lobo Mountain. That's what you see. It won't be long now before there's snow on Lobo Mountain, too."

"Aspens," I repeated. "They're lovely."

"Just came out in the last few nights, and only to stay a few weeks."

I began reading again. But my mind was full of what Sebastian has said. Soon there would be snow on Lobo Mountain. I doubted that I would be there to see it. In a little while, I was sure, the evil charade in which I was an actress must come to an end. I could hear my own voice as from a distance. It rolled out smoothly, evenly, intoning the words. Yet my mind went about its own business, tiptoed delicately past fear, asked quick questions, found answers only to reject them, sorted and chose, searching for a truth it couldn't uncover.

Sebastian sighed. "I think that's enough, girl."

I looked up at him. "Your mind isn't on it."

"Neither is yours, Robin."

Henley stirred, a small soundless movement, which I saw from the corner of my eye.

"Would you like a nap before lunch, Sebastian?" I asked.

He nodded. "I suppose."

I took the pipe from his big hand, found the light coverlet, and spread it over him.

"Service." Sebastian gave me a sudden grin. "I could stand one of those small sweet smiles along with it."

My throat was too tight. I could feel a sob growing inside me. I made myself grin back.

"Sebastian, you're trying to flatter me."

"Not too much; that's for sure, girl."

I was at the door when he asked, "Annetta and Jamie in town again?"

I turned back and found that small silent Henley was right on my heels. We wavered back and forth trying not to bump into each other.

Sebastian laughed softly. "You got a good routine there."

Henley grunted, made a wide circle around me, and then went out.

"They in town?" Sebastian repeated.

"Yes, I imagine so."

"Restless," Sebastian said. "The both of them. It's contagious, maybe. Annetta never used to be restless. That talk about San Francisco—you notice it?"

"Eighteen is a restless age, Sebastian."

"For some people, every age is restless. I remember her mother——"

"Rose," I said softly.

"Yes. Rose." He sighed, turned his head away. "But Annetta never was restless before. That's the thing." Sebastian went on thoughtfully, "So why should she be restless now?"

I didn't answer, though I knew why.

"San Francisco," he said, and grunted a soft refusal of the idea. He didn't need me to tell him, I realized. He was working around to the truth himself.

It was Jamie, of course. Jamie painting a picture of

excitement that would appeal to any teen-ager. And I knew why he was doing it.

Sebastian grunted again. "But don't you worry about it, Robin. I want you to be happy here. That's what I really want. I want you to be so happy here that your happiness will spill over into Jamie, so he'll stay home, and be the man he can be. Or, if not that, then there's Austin. And the plane to bring you both back and forth —I'm an old man, dreaming, I guess. But I want to see my grandchildren before I die. That's not asking too much of this life, is it? Just to see my grandchildren for a little while?"

I changed the subject. "Sebastian, if you're going to nap before lunch, you'd better start now."

"Now don't get on a high horse, girl. I know I'm minding your business, and I'm doing it on purpose. But I figure it's my business, too."

I laughed helplessly, but I felt more like crying.

"It's a compliment to you. Don't you know that, girl?"

"I know," I said. "I understand."

"We're all changing," he went on in his slow breathless way. "Do you feel it? No. You never knew Michael before. He's a shadow of himself. Since Ayren died— like me when Rose went away—but, at least, I had the children, something to go on for. And Michael—no, he's not the man he was. Jamie was born restless, like I told you once, crying for his mother, crying his way into this world to scream for Angelina, and, of course, he couldn't ever have her——"

"Sebastian," I whispered, blinking back tears.

The old man continued, "Still, there's something new in his attitude. I feel it. I pray he'll never hurt you, girl. I'll pray forever that he'll value you as you should be valued. Did you know I had nearly given up on Jamie? But he married you. The good part of him wanted you, Robin. I knew then I could still dare hope."

I wanted to cry out, "No, Sebastian, don't let me fool you that way." It was, in a way, harder to remain silent, than to speak.

He went on, "And you, you, yourself—you're changing, too. It's this house, I know. It must be—could this house be cursed?"

He had raised himself on an elbow.

"That's no way to rest," I said reproachfully, trying to smile. "Going on about curses——"

But he shook his head, went on. "I never believed it, you know. For all that's happened here, I never believed it. But still——" He paused, a grin touched the corners of his bluish lips. "Girl, I see you going pale before my eyes. Don't you know you mustn't ever listen to an old man before he falls asleep? The foolish things he says, like wake-up nightmares." He stretched out again, let lined lids fall over sparkling dark blue. "But you tell Annetta for me that when she comes back, I want a chess game."

"I'll tell her," I promised.

I went out into the silent hall. Henley was standing there, just standing. I knew he had been listening.

"This house *is* cursed," he said, as I went by.

I didn't answer him. I felt his eyes follow me, step by step, as I climbed the wide stairs.

Maria was dusting the wide oval banisters. She paused, the old-fashioned brush, like an Indian chieftain's headdress, rippled somehow in the still air.

"Are they back?" Maria asked.

"I haven't seen them yet."

"It is impossible," she said somberly. "You cannot say *no* to everything. But it is not good for her to run each day to Cromwell Crossing with Jamie. There is nothing amusing here for her to do."

"I know," I said.

"I have said she must not climb in the caves. I have

said she must not wander in the fields, nor drive the car, nor——"

"But why, Maria?"

"It is not safe. She can be hurt." Maria's broad dusky face was expressionless. "She can be hurt so badly. We must take care of our Annetta." She smiled suddenly, her face full of the warmth of love. "And we must take care of our Robin, too. Our small Robin."

I touched her plump back, and started toward the south wing. Michael's door was open. As I passed it, he appeared as if he had been waiting for the sound of my voice, appeared suddenly as if he had been watching for me."

"Are they home?" he asked.

"Annetta and Jamie?"

He jerked his head in a wordless nod. His pale expressionless eyes looked into my face, then slid away. His dark hair was ruffled, as though his hands had plowed through it time and time again. I supposed he had been working, perhaps making his phone calls, reading reports. I couldn't pretend to understand the Cromwell affairs; they didn't matter to me anyway.

"I don't think so," I said. "At least, I haven't seen or heard them yet."

Without a word, he disappeared inside. Then I saw him again, his back to me, wide shoulders taut, looking out of the window that faced the parking area at the back of the house.

The aura of stillness that had seemed to surround the house before was gone now. I felt an uneasiness throb and pulse through the quiet halls and echo through me.

I found myself breathing carefully as I went into my suite. Maria had been there. The rooms were straightened and aired, the furniture freshly waxed. A small vase held two tiny rosebuds. I knew that somewhere in the mass of greenery below the window wall in the kitchen, I would find some tiny roses blooming because of her love and care.

The curtains were blowing at the wide doors of the bedroom window. They billowed and draped and slid over the green chaise on flutters of damp wind. It was as if streamers of gray cloud were flowing in with each movement. I closed the window. As the curtains settled, I saw a bundle of pale-blue silk against the dark green of the chaise.

I stared at it, my breath frozen in my throat. I stared at it for long moments before I dared reach out and pick it up with trembling fingers. It was my favorite dress, the one I had worn the night Sebastian gave me the emeralds as a wedding gift. The night that now seemed so far away in time as to be almost a dream. The night that I had known in my heart that neither emeralds, nor money, nor all my childish dreams, could excuse what Jamie and I were doing in deceiving Sebastian.

I held the dress up, knowing, knowing even before I looked, what I would find. The long tears, the cuts, slashes, rips, were intended not for the tender silk, but for me. Just as the thin silver knife rammed through the potato had not been meant for the potato itself, but for me.

I heard a movement outside and flung the window open again. Henley was there; a large watering can stood before him.

"Everything that lives needs tending," he explained. Wordlessly, I turned away, hearing his mumbled, *"If they're to survive, they need tending."*

I sank down on the chaise, holding the tattered dress against me, cuddling it as if I could assuage its pain, as if it could feel pain.

The gray stillness in the beautiful room mocked me; the two tiny roses in their small vase looked absurd.

Maria had been in the hallway. Michael in his room.

Henley outside on the balcony. Any of these three could have thrust scissors through the thin silk, imagining, with pleasure, my body inside of it.

And then I remembered that I hadn't been in my room since before Jamie and Annetta left the house. So either of them could have done it too.

The hall was empty now, but Michael's door was open, and he was still at his window.

"Michael," I croaked.

He turned.

I held out the torn dress, wondering why I had come to him.

He was across the room in a limping rush. He pulled the dress from my fingers, held it up, staring at the long slashes in the fabric. His hands knotted around it, then jerked, and it seemed to cry out as it broke apart in his hands. His pale-gray eyes came up to mine.

"Did you do it?" I whispered.

"I?" He seemed bewildered, but then the curtain fell across his face. He asked bleakly, "When did you find this, Robin?"

"Just now."

"Now?" He opened his hands, let the pieces fall to the floor. He turned his back, went to the window.

"You, Henley, Maria——" I said to his rigid back.

"Or Jamie, or Annetta," he retorted, reminding me that I had thought of them already.

Without answering, I caught up the destroyed dress. It seemed to burn my fingers as I edged out of the room.

Maria was in the kitchen. Seeing the rags I held, she asked, "What, Robin?"

I let her take the shreds from me; pale silk like blue ribbons fluttered in her fingers. She examined them. A look of pain, of fright, seemed to put new shadows into her small old face, withering the plump dusky cheeks, narrowing the dark slanted eyes.

"A child's game—again——" she whispered.

But I saw the furtive movement of her fingers as she crossed herself.

"It is only a child's game, Robin," she repeated, making me a promise with her tone of voice.

I shook my head. A car door slammed outside. Jamie and Annetta. I started out, thinking to deliver Sebastian's message—Annetta was to play chess with him when she returned.

But she and Jamie burst in, and I forgot the message. Even if I had remembered, I wouldn't have delivered it.

The two of them had been in town too long, and I knew what they had been doing. Not driving too fast on the curved roads, not hanging around the drugstore, not visiting with Belinda Robard. They'd been in the café, feeding quarters into the juke box and drinking beer together. Annetta growing more and more gay, her head not accustomed to so much beer. Jamie, egging her on, and opening doors to a world she had never even dreamed about, much less wanted, until he brought that world to her, glowing and bright and inviting with a promise the wind-eroded mountains of the high country could never offer.

Annetta, her high young voice more shrill than ever, her creamy pale skin flushed now and sweating, her shining black eyes full of red glints, brushed past me as if I were not there, crying, "Jamie, remember now."

And Jamie, chuckling, his face, too, aglow, said, "You had better sack out in the nursery before lunch, sister mine. You've had a snootful and it shows on you."

She went dancing out of the kitchen, past Maria, crying, "Hi, hi," and yawned widely before she skipped on.

Maria said softly, "Oh, you, Jamie, you!" Her breath hissed, an audible disapproval.

I turned to Jamie. "That's disgusting," I said in a furious whisper.

"What?"

"You know."

The sullen look was gone from him. Jamie gave me an open boyish smile, an innocent smile, the kind I recognized from those days when he had sought to win me in a mock courtship that had ended in the revealing frankness which had made me trust him. This time I was more wary.

"To do that to Annetta," I explained. "You know you let her have too much to drink. You did it on purpose too."

"So she had a few. So what?"

Maria had left us, retreating to her room. I wondered what she was doing there. I wondered if she had knelt to pray for all of us before the carved *santos* on the mantel. I wondered if she were whispering pleading words into the incense-sweet air.

Jamie went on. "I don't want any lectures, Robin, honey." He chuckled. "I've had a snootful. I never dreamed when I took you on——"

"I never dreamed you'd stoop so low."

"You ought to have known I'd do anything." He shrugged. "More fool you, if you didn't."

I trailed him up to our suite. Inside, I said, "Jamie, if you force me to——"

He grinned still, but something evil peeped at me from his pale-blue eyes. "I don't believe I'll worry what you do any more, Robin."

I knew then that he had either teased or tickled Annetta into telling him where the jewels had been hidden. I could imagine her, fuzzy with beer, looking around at the others in the café, then, leaning close to Jamie's laughing face—that boyish brotherly face—saying, "Yes, I know, Jamie. And if you'd stayed home with me instead of running off and leaving me, then you'd know, too." And later, even more fuzzy with more beer, I could hear her saying indignantly, "Of course, I know. Sebastian's smart. But I'm smart, too. So I watched him one time—I saw——"

I couldn't imagine more than that. I couldn't follow through to picture what she had seen, what she knew.

But I was certain Jamie had pried the secret out of her. I would no longer see him prowling the old house speculatively eyeing the fireplaces; no longer hear his footsteps in the dead of night as he crept through the door behind the damask wall hangings to climb the narrow steps to the old playroom in the eaves.

Jamie's mood confirmed my suspicions. He was relaxed, but unable to hide his jubilation. I knew he was already making plans, walking under the twinkling lights of San Francisco, climbing the windy hills, away from the prison of the house that had been his home—but never his home in his heart—away from the place where he had cried for the mother he had never had.

A part of me ached for him, for what he had become. Despite my sympathy for him, I couldn't excuse Jamie for what he planned to do to Sebastian, any more than I could excuse myself for having come to Cromwell Crossing with him.

I had made up my mind to stop Jamie if I could. It was the only reason I had stayed on in the house where a shadow hung over me, threatening, fearsome—a shadow that I couldn't see, yet knew was there. I could still hear the voice of the young blond clerk in the drugstore saying, "Cromwell Castle sure is hard on the wives." Rose, Ayren, and now me. . . .

I watched Jamie all that day. I dogged his steps until he laughed at me, "Suddenly playing the sweet bride again, Robin?"

"It's not such a bad idea, is it?" I asked wistfully. "Maybe Sebastian could still be persuaded——?"

Jamie grinned. "It's too late, Robin, honey. Though I

admit, if you tried real hard, you maybe could make the bride bit attractive."

"Jamie!"

"Then don't play the nut. You're not going to stop me." But he was still smiling, still boyish—as if nothing could spoil his mood.

I remember the false air of gaiety that touched all of us as we sat down to dinner that night. Sebastian had suggested wine to Henley, who made a great show of serving it, filling each crystal goblet to the brim while Maria served us.

Annetta giggled happily. She was still in what I thought of as her "San Francisco mood." Her bright eyes were made up with liner and shadow; her lips brilliantly red. She wore one of the Neiman-Marcus dresses, an off-white.

She preened herself like a delighted child, in spite of her sophisticated look, when Sebastian said with approval, "That's my girl, pretty as a picture. We ought to have asked Ned and Belinda up to see the sight."

Annetta shook her head, flinging back her dark curls, and her diamond earrings glittered and danced, just as her dreams must have glittered and danced before her eyes.

Jamie said, "I doubt that the Cromwells deserve such luck—two glamour girls at one table."

Sebastian grinned, "Why, we do, boy! And why not? We Cromwells make our own luck."

I couldn't look at Sebastian. Inwardly, I winced at what he'd said. It was almost as if he were giving Jamie a kind of permission. Michael moved restlessly as Sebastian went on, talking about other Cromwells, the things they had done. I had a quick glimpse of Jamie's eyes, sardonic, knowing, teasing, on me. I looked away.

Only Michael and I seemed to be untouched by that false air of gaiety. He was silent, bleak as always. I wondered what he was thinking behind those pale eyes of his, behind that judging, measuring look.

I thought of his hands, fingers like steel on my arms, holding himself in, saying, "You little fool! Do you think I'm the one? That I'd ever hurt you?" I thought of his hands ripping the pale-blue silk of my torn dress, ripping it in two as if he were tearing me in two. I thought, then, of that moment when he had held me, that moment on the porch, when the two of us were so plainly melting together, holding back, yet melting toward each other, until Jamie's sour voice thrust us apart. I told myself I must forget that moment. For, soon, I would be going away. I would never see Michael Cromwell again.

Dinner was finally over. Sebastian, much to my relief, didn't invite Ned and Belinda out for coffee.

Annetta and her father settled down in the study over a chessboard. Jamie and Michael nursed brandies and watched them. I went to the window, and my eyes followed the odd muffled glow of the sun as it sank, spilling weird combinations of colors behind the curtain of the heavy overcast.

Behind me, Sebastian said once, twice, three times, "Annetta, keep your mind on the game." Annetta laughed shrilly in answer.

Henley passed the window, peered in, then passed again, soundless as always, his glasses glinting with reflections of pink light, his small face eyeless and tipped to one side.

At last, the long slow quiet evening ended.

I went upstairs with Jamie.

Knowing it was useless, I tried one more time to dissuade him. "Jamie, you could give it a little more time. I think Sebastian's ready to think it over."

"You don't know old Sebastian as well as I do." Jamie grinned. "Having second thoughts?"

I ignored that. I wouldn't let myself argue with him.

I asked, "Don't you see how much better it would be?"

"Robin, honey, you're so transparent—playing for time——"

He unbuttoned his shirt, yawned, stretched.

"But don't you see?" I pleaded.

Jamie kept smiling, but his voice was hard. "Can't you take a hint? I'm getting ready for bed." He made the next words softer, insinuating, "Or maybe you're giving me the hint? Maybe you want to stay here, with me, maybe you——"

Disgusted, I turned on my heel, went into the bedroom. I grabbed his pillow, the coverlet off the bed, brought them into the sitting room, and flung them at him. Jamie laughed softly as I retreated to the bedroom and closed the door firmly between us.

Suddenly the room was stifling. My cheeks burned. My hands shook as I opened the double doors, let the breeze blow through my pixie-cut hair.

The overcast had finally thinned. A narrow moon hung over the valley. The house was still as I thought of undressing, of hiding in bed. But I was sure now that Jamie knew where the Galveston jewels were concealed. And, knowing Jamie, I was sure, too, that he wouldn't wait—he wouldn't wait a moment longer than he had to. He would get them and then drive away, leaving me to face Sebastian.

I sat on the edge of the bed, braced, listening, staring into the darkness. I heard Jamie yawn, heard the whisper of the sofa as he lay down. I heard the click of the lamp as he turned it off.

I got up. For a long while, I watched the crescent moon rise and glide across the sky and begin to sink again. I went back to the bed, and kicked off my shoes, and, still dressed, I leaned against the headboard.

I don't know how much time passed while I forced my

eyes to stay open, forced my senses to remain alert—
waiting as the house waited.

Then I heard the whisper of the sofa again—the
sounds that meant Jamie had gotten up. I heard the soft
brushing of his shoes on the thick rug, and the faintest
complaint of a doorknob being turned.

I jumped up, hurried into the sitting room. It was already empty, the door ajar. I stared at it, at the shadows
beyond.

I remembered the last time I had rushed from that
room, had rushed wildly into those same shadows, and I
had tripped, floundering on empty air above the steep
steps.

I remembered, and I knew that Jamie might be somewhere out there, waiting for me. Yet I had to stop him
if I could. I didn't think. I pushed the door wide, and
went down the dark hall as silently as Henley ever had.
At the top of the stairs, I paused. But then, from below,
I heard a sound. I knew it must be Jamie.

I ran then. I ran down the steps, through the dark,
clinging with sliding damp fingers to the curved banisters; ran toward the faint pink glow of the night light in
the hall below.

Chapter NINETEEN

JAMIE WAS there, crouched beneath the dark ancestral
portraits of Cromwells. His face was faintly pink in the
light, a devil's face, intense with cunning and greed. As
I reached the last landing, he bent over the huge potted
plant outside Sebastian's closed door.

Quickly, silently, Jamie clawed the dry soil, flinging it away through hooked fingers.

I whispered a soundless, "No, Jamie. No, please—you can't——" and started for him.

It was like some wild, half-forgotten nightmare. Time faltered and died and began again. What seemed to have been hours could only have been moments, just moments fleeting by, as I ran the rest of the way down the carpeted stairs.

And, as I ran, I saw a shadow break and move and sidle along the wall to leap at Jamie. Pink light suddenly reflected back from rimless glasses like tiny whips of lightning in the dark.

Henley cried in a thin desperate voice, "No, no. You can't have them. The Galveston stones are mine. They're mine. I earned them, I tell you. I, not you! I was the one! Me! Nobody Henley himself, from that scrub farm in Texas. Me, Nobody Henley! I hijacked them from the looters. It was stealing from thieves, not stealing at all."

"They're mine now," Jamie retorted.

But Henley went on in a burning whisper, "I got shot for my trouble. Me, Henley, with the bullet in my chest. That's why Sebastian brought me up here. Me, and the Galveston stones—the both of us to cool off."

"Then, cool off," Jamie rasped.

"I was scared, Jamie. You can't think how scared. All that wind, the trees splintering down in the night. Sebastian knew the men and the place and the time, but I was the one there, and I got the stones. And here, stuck away in nowhere, fit for nothing but serving, and waiting for the stones to be mine again—mine—Henley's——"

The bell-clear words poured out of Henley, who so rarely spoke, from catfooted Henley, as he flung himself on Jamie, clung to Jamie's shoulders.

Jamie, bigger, stronger, faster, flung Henley away, but the small man was instantly back on his feet, tearing at

Jamie's shoulders again, while the words spilled out, in a desperate whisper.

"I knew you were up to something. You and the girl. You had to be. You always were. Didn't I get you out of enough jams to know you? So I figured it out. I knew I'd never scare you off. But the girl—yes—she was scared when she came. So I tried to scare her more. To make her take you away with her. I wouldn't ever hurt her. No, not me. Henley doesn't hurt people. But just to give a warning. The knife in the potato. The ripped dress. Just to scare her so she'd take you away."

Jamie straightened up, twisted, swearing under his breath. His fist slashed in a terrible backhand at Henley's face.

Henley dropped like a broken toy, rolled, was still.

Jamie crouched over the pot again, sifting the dry dirt.

And I, gasping, was finally at his side. I heard the sudden swift intake of his breath. He raised his hand. Sweet-smelling earth, a familiar scent, clung to his fingers, to the sack he held.

He smiled at me triumphantly. "You see? I have it. My life, right here in my hand."

"Jamie, you mustn't. You'll break Sebastian's heart," I pleaded.

Beyond Jamie, I saw Henley. The small man pushed himself carefully to his knees, felt the rug around him, then gently set cracked glasses on his nose before rising gracelessly to his feet.

My hand was on Jamie's arm. I turned him, moved with him, so that I stood between him and Henley. All the while, breathlessly, I whispered, "Listen, both of you. You can't do this to Sebastian. Don't make any noise, he'll hear you. Don't do anything that will hurt——" and I was saying more, more, when the overhead chandeliers flashed on, drowning us in rose-colored light, throwing huge thin shadows on the walls, shadows that broke and lunged and swelled.

Annetta was on the stairs above us. Annetta, crying in a shrill high voice, "Jamie, you can't do that to me."

We looked up at her, straining, disbelieving—Jamie, Henley, and I. We stared at her in a moment of silence as thick as a shroud.

She held the gun that was usually on Sebastian's mantel. I had time, in that long still moment, to wonder how she had gotten it.

"We were going together, you and me, for a little while, and then we'd come back, you promised, to be with Sebastian and Michael. But you tricked me. And it was all for her."

"We are," Jamie said. "I just came to get the stones, and then I was going to——"

"No. You tricked me, Jamie. You're dressed, and so is she. You tricked me for her."

The gun moved, swayed, centered then on me, centered steadily, while I stared at her, still not believing what I saw.

Annetta's young face was lined, hardened, the shining black eyes glittering with a malice I had seen once before when Jamie first introduced me to her—the night when I came to Cromwell Crossing that now seemed so long ago.

"Your fault," Annetta said, her voice becoming hoarse, thick. "Yours, Bobby. You took them all away from me. Jamie, Sebastian, Michael. They're mine. But you took them away. Small you, little you, graceful you. Bobby!"

I was frozen, sheathed in ice, so that even my heart seemed to slow, to restrain its beat, but the long still moment, suddenly shattered by her words, became time racing, plunging ahead, like a movie reel played too fast.

Beyond Annetta, I saw feet, moving slowly, silently,

long legs, a slight limp, a lean taut body, a hand raised in warning, and then, finally, Michael's face, emerging from the shadows into the pink glow. Five steps behind her, then four, then three. . . .

"We are the Cromwells," Annetta said. "We belong together. You can't take my men away from me."

I felt Jamie's sudden movement at my side at the same time that I saw Michael's lunge. Then the room spun around me as I fell under the shove of Jamie's hands.

I heard a flat hard sound.

Jamie screamed, "Annetta!" and wavered and fell, while Michael's arms went around a writhing, shrieking Annetta, and his hands sought the gun that she waved just beyond his reach.

Henley, mumbling to himself, hugged the wall.

Maria, suddenly plunging in from the dark living room, threw herself at Annetta and Michael and was kicked back. She fell heavily on the stairs, her stolid face shining with tears.

I dragged myself up, crawled to Jamie. He was still clutching the sack. There was blood on his lips, blood on his white shirt. His fingers tore at the sack, finally opened it. Bright stones, spilled chips of light, a sparkling waterfall fell across his blood-wet chest. "Almost," he whispered. "Almost got there, Robin."

"Jamie!" It was Annetta. She was frozen in Michael's arms, frozen and unmoving, her black eyes staring down at us. "Jamie?"

Then, as Michael's fingers closed around the gun, she came to life. She jerked away, suddenly screaming, as if some thin raveling thread within her had broken.

Still clenching the gun, Annetta spun free of Michael, jumped the steps, and tore free of Maria's clutching fingers, to race down the hall to the valley door. Then, she paused, turned back.

"Jamie?" she asked, her voice high and clear again.

I could hear his breath, a bubbling, frightening sound. "Annetta, he needs a doctor," I cried.

There was a sudden froth of white at her lips. Her head went up. Her eyes flashed black fire. "Your fault, Bobby. Yours, and Ayren's, and in the beginning, there was Rose. Yes, Rose, beautiful Rose." Annetta went on, her voice suddenly soft, husky. "Do you remember, our beautiful Rose, how she was?" She paused. Her face crumpled and sagged, and bright tears stained her cheeks.

I took an involuntary step forward.

"No," she said, still in a husky voice. "No, Bobby."

Michael, now at the bottom of the stairs, moved, and again, though not looking at him, Annetta said, "No," with the gun centered, steady, aiming at me.

At my feet, Jamie was still now, but Maria bent over him, whispering a prayer.

"Beautiful Rose," Annetta sneered. "That was the beginning. I read the letters she wrote to that man. To her lover. She was going to leave and take me away. Do you remember how it was? I couldn't let her do that. I belong to you, and you belong to me. So I took her up to the cave. I left her in the caves one sunny afternoon. I left her there screaming for help! I came down and packed a suitcase, and brought it back that night. She wasn't screaming any more. She's still here at Cromwell Crossing. Sometimes, I think I can still hear her screaming." Annetta paused. "And then we were so happy, Michael. Remember how it was? You and me and Jamie and Sebastian. The four Cromwells. But you spoiled it. You brought Ayren here."

"Annetta stop," Michael said.

If she heard him, she gave no sign. She went on, "Listen, Michael, why did you bring Ayren? What did you need her for? She took over, tall and sure of herself, and just like Rose all over again. She spoiled it all. She had you, but she had to have Jamie, too, and you know what she did with him. And Sebastian thought she was a queen. Rotten Ayren. I had to get rid of her. I didn't know you'd drive her to town that day. I saved you, didn't I, Michael? I cracked the steering pin so she'd wreck the car, but you were trapped—and I saved you. Then Sebastian got sick, and you went away, and soon Jamie went, too. I thought God was punishing me. When Jamie called to say he was coming home, I knew it was all right. I was forgiven." She shook her head, flinging back the shiny black curls. "I didn't know about Bobby. He didn't tell me."

Sebastian, speaking slowly, saving his breath, cut in, "That's enough now, Annetta," and held out his hand to her. "I'll have my gun now."

But Annetta, moving closer to the door, shook her head again.

I wondered how long Sebastian had been there, what he had heard.

Annetta went on. "That morning I saw her near the balcony; I didn't even have to think." She made a gesture with her hand. "Over went the planter. Crash! Scream!" She laughed. But she continued, sober again. "It missed her. And somehow Michael was there, home again with me, so I knew I was right. I'd have to try again. I remembered Rose. Rose and Robin. They would be company for each other in the cave. I took Bobby with me, but it didn't work out right. How did you know, Michael? Why did you follow? Why did you care so much? And that wire. You found that wire, too, didn't you, Michael? You found it, took it away. So Bobby stayed on."

Michael took another step.

"I'll shoot her," Annetta said. "Move away so I can shoot her, Michael."

His arms closed around me, held me, melting the sheath of ice in which I had been enwrapped.

"You'll have to kill both of us, Annetta," he said softly. "Robin and me, together."

She edged the door open. The gun shook in her hand. "It's all her fault. All of it. Even the jewels. Jamie and I were going to go away together for a little while; then she'd leave, too. Then we'd all be together again—the Cromwells, just us. But Jamie was going to take her, not me, and Michael would leave again. It can't be that way. We four have to be together. That's the only way anybody'd love me."

Sebastian, leaning against the wall, slid toward her. "Annetta—baby——"

She steadied the gun. "Michael, you want her, too, don't you? I've seen you look at her. I see how you're holding her."

"We all love you," Sebastian said softly. "Baby, we always have and always will."

Annetta stood still, staring at me, at Michael. Her black eyes widened until they seemed to fill her white face. Suddenly, she screamed, "I can't and won't!" She flung the gun down.

The wild girl twisted from Sebastian's reaching hand, cried, "You gave her the emeralds, Sebastian." She shoved the door back, and dashed outside. Michael and I raced after her.

We heard the clatter of her footsteps on the stone terrace, saw her slim shadow duck and twist and writhe as she ran to the edge, teetered there frantically, and then disappeared as she went over into the treetops.

There was a crash, the splintering of wood, crackles and rips; then the slow dwindling thuds of matter and rocks settling below.

I remembered Jamie telling me what would happen to

me if he threw me over the terrace into the treetops—
the awful picture he had drawn.

"God help her," Michael whispered, touching my tear-
wet face tenderly as I backed away.

The windows of the house were ablaze with light now.
As I followed Michael in, I could hear Maria, her voice
soft, speaking on the telephone.

Sebastian was on the floor beside Jamie, a limp, blood-
stained Jamie who would never smile again. Sebastian
mumbled, blue-lipped, pasty, "I guess he was a Cromwell after all."

Henley, whispering to himself, peering through his
cracked glasses, pounced on the shining stones that were
scattered around Jamie. Pounced on them, and whispered, and dropped them one by one into the blood-dark
sack.

Sebastian sighed, "I said I got them cheap, the Galveston stones. I said they cost little—but they cost a lot,
it seems. One son, one daughter, too." His head sank to
his chest. "Take them, Henley. You want them, they're
yours. Take those damn stones, and yourself, and get out
of here."

Then, reaching out blindly, he touched Jamie's face,
and gasped, and fell sideways.

Henley, still maundering, still clasping the sack in
his hand, helped Michael and me get Sebastian into
bed.

While we were waiting for Ned Robard to get there,
watching Sebastian and trying to breathe for him to ease
his laborious gasps, Henley slipped away. I never knew
when he left.

Michael and I stayed with Sebastian, waiting, not looking at each other, not talking.

I don't know about Michael, but I couldn't even think
—except in small snatches of prayer—while Sebastian
gasped broken words.

I heard him say: "Why? What did I do? Was it pride? The portraits—two gone—my own—my own——"

I found myself weeping. For him, for Jamie, for Annetta. . . .

Michael said gently, "He'll be all right, Robin. He's tough as leather."

Later, Ned Robard said the same thing. He came out of Sebastian's room gray-faced, his bald head shining with sweat, his oddly askew face more twisted than ever with a mixture of sorrow and relief that was instantly mirrored on Belinda's.

The couple had come in together. Ned, bounding ahead, crying, "What's this Maria says? What's this?" as he flung the big door open, nearly bowling Maria over. "What's this?" Ned said for the third time, his voice suddenly hushed as he knelt beside Jamie. He instantly straightened to demand, "And Sebastian?"

Belinda, who had been just behind him, seemed frozen. Her high color was faded, her quick breathless words stilled.

She looked from me to Michael, asking a thousand questions with her eyes, but voicing none of them, as Michael took Ned in to Sebastian's room.

Maria had gently covered Jamie's body with Sebastian's coverlet.

"Poor child," Belinda whispered. "Poor children," and took me into her arms.

Chapter *TWENTY*

IT WAS nearly dawn. A rim of pale blue edged the far side of the valley. I could hear the fading sound of the Robards' car as it circled down the mountain, and see the faint glint of its light flickering in the trees.

The house was very still. Still now after the questions, the exploding flashbulbs, the stamp of booted feet. Still now after the hard flat sound of the gun, Jamie's bubbling breath and Annetta's shriek.

The whole night had the quality of a receding dream. Yet it had all been real. I had seen Jamie's body wrapped in blankets and carried away, while Belinda wept and held me. I had seen Michael and Ned go with the troopers—go out into the still night, the impossible night—to circle the house, carrying ropes, to climb down and down past the slender treetops to the boulders below. I had seen them return bearing Annetta's broken body, with Michael gently holding her limp hand beneath the stained sheets.

Ned, as county coroner, wrote his report leaning on the wide banister under the pink glow of the main hall. "Accidental shooting," he said. And then, "Suicide while of unsound mind. Remorse." He and the state troopers looked at each other and nodded in unspoken agreement.

Now they were all gone. The other cars first, then the Robards'.

"Sebastian's sleeping," Ned had said before they left.

"A natural sleep, a healing sleep, a forgetting sleep." He turned his gaze from Michael to me. "And now you two must do the same."

But Michael had gone in to look at Sebastian, to see if Maria needed anything for the rest of the night, and I had gone out to the porch to watch the last of the cars go down the mountain.

When the lights disappeared, I went inside. In the pink glow of the chandelier, I listened to the stillness of the house. We were alone. Sebastian and Michael and Maria and I. But I didn't belong there. I was the stranger.

I took a deep breath and started for the steps, looking ahead to the shadows on the upper floor, wondering if I dared brave them. Yet I recognized in that moment a difference in the silence. It was as if the house had settled back, relaxed.

Michael came out of Sebastian's wing. He bent, touched the scattering of dirt on the rug, the overturned potted plant. Then he straightened up.

"Wait, Robin. We need some coffee. Come into the kitchen," Michael invited.

I followed him through the dark rooms.

I offered to help him, but he waved me aside. I sat at the big round table, watching sunrise touch the wide windows, warm the garden Maria had grown beneath them, slide a glinting touch over the copper pots on the wall. I felt as if I were taking a last long look at a place I loved.

Michael limped to the table with steaming coffee cups. He sat opposite me.

"I can understand if you blame me," he said heavily. "I should have been able to stop it, Robin."

Suddenly I had to ask him, to know. "Michael, why did you come back to Cromwell Crossing as soon as you heard that Jamie had . . . ?" I found that I couldn't say it, couldn't repeat the lie. I couldn't make myself say: "When you heard that Jamie had married me." Instead, I changed it. I said, "—when you heard that Jamie had brought me home with him?"

"I had to, Robin. That's the whole thing."

"But why? It must have been terrible for you. After Ayren—I mean——"

"Robin, I didn't leave Sebastian after Ayren's death because the memory of it was too much for me. I knew about her and Jamie. She was like Annetta. She had to have it all, all the love around and more. I left because of how I felt about Annetta. I couldn't forget my suspicions. You see, when the car went wild and crashed, I was pinned, but conscious. Annetta was there almost immediately. I heard her talking to Ayren, though Ayren was already dead. I heard Annetta saying, 'I hate you, and I've won.' "

I drew a deep aching breath. "Oh, Michael——"

"I couldn't be sure. The car was completely wrecked and disposed of by the time my leg was healed enough for me to get around. But the suspicions were in my mind. I had to get away. I came back to be sure that nothing happened to Jamie's bride. When the planter fell that morning, I was sure my suspicions had been right. That's why I tried to persuade you to go away."

"I didn't understand."

"Maria had her own fears. She knew Annetta, loved Annetta, so well. She was as determined as I to stop Annetta, save her from harming herself or anyone else —yet to protect Sebastian at the same time."

"So she told you we were going into the caves? And you followed?"

"I was behind you all the time except for those moments when you stumbled on Rose. I was stunned, afraid the news might kill Sebastian. I couldn't let you tell anyone. I tried to talk Sebastian into giving Jamie the settlement, but it was like trying to move a stone wall." Michael sighed. "I wanted Jamie to get that money, figuring he'd go away, and you with him, as soon as he did. He was always a bit of a twister, Jamie." Michael looked at me bleakly. "You could have chosen more wisely."

"Michael——" I was going to tell him the truth then and there, to rip off the false wedding band I wore and fling it away, but he interrupted.

"Never mind." He shook his dark head wearily. His pale eyes touched my gaze, then slid away. "I oughtn't to have said that. I just want you to know that I did try to protect you. I was always watching, listening. I couldn't explain it to you, warn you any more than I did, because——" He shrugged. "I guess I took chances I shouldn't have taken. Not with your life, Robin. Forgive me, if you can. Try to remember that Annetta was my sister. In spite of everything, I loved her, too."

"I loved her, too."
I heard those words over and over again in my mind for the next few days. I thought of them, cherished them, and told myself to forget them. I was the stranger in Cromwell Crossing, and soon I would have to leave.

It was a bright morning. We drove to town together: Sebastian, still gray-faced and blue-lipped, but showing the resiliency he'd always had, Maria, weeping, and Michael, grim. I wore a dark-gray linen dress and a tiny hat, feeling like the impostor I was, for pretending to be a widow.

We went to the chapel, where a brief service was read over the three coffins. Yes, the three. For Rose was buried in the Cromwell family plot beside Annetta and Jamie that day. Michael had led the long sorry trek

through the caves and brought Rose out into the sunshine again for a brief time.

We were at the cemetery, standing beside the open
graves that were surrounded by splintered wooden
crosses, fine stone markers, and withered flowers on the
dusty ground, when a small figure slid in beside Sebastian—a small figure with eyes blanked out by glasses
that twinkled in the sun.

Henley whispered, "I had to come," to no one in
particular, but it was meant for everyone there.

He stayed with us, with the Robards and a few people
from town, and later, at the car, Sebastian raised his
weathered, tear-blurred face, and said, "Henley, I want
to thank you."

"Then let me come home," Henley mumbled. "Here.
Take the stones. I don't want them. I only want to come
home. How did I know that would happen? Eight years,
I spent there, my best eight, and always thinking of the
stones. But when I had them, they were nothing to me
but shining death, Sebastian."

"You wanted them, now you've got them," Sebastian
said.

But Maria whispered, "No, no. Forgive one, forgive
all."

Sebastian hesitated, then nodded, "All right. Come on
home, Henley." But he waved the small sack away.

Hesitantly, Henley offered it to Michael. He, too,
shook his head in refusal.

"I'll send them to Galveston," Henley mumbled.
"Charities can use them." He climbed into the car,
nodded, and squeezed the small sack. "Yes, back to Galveston to do some good."

It was later—in the afternoon. I had noticed, since
returning, the change in the house. Sorrow was there,
yes, but terror no longer. The secrets of Cromwell

Crossing were secrets no more. Except for one. I myself carried the burden of it. And I knew that before I went away, I would have to lay that burden down.

I couldn't put off the reckoning. Sebastian was in his study with Michael.

"Come on, girl," Sebastian said. "Come and be with us. We thought you might be sleeping."

"I couldn't sleep," I told him.

"Then sit."

I perched on the edge of the big desk. I braced myself. I looked carefully, exclusively, at Sebastian, saying, "I am going up to pack now. I'm leaving, Sebastian. Today."

There was a moment of startled silence, then Sebastian protested, "But you can't do that, girl. It's the craziest thing I ever heard of. You belong here. You were Jamie's wife——" He paused. "Unless you hate us all. Unless you feel you can't bear it. And if that's the case, well, then, we'll settle you someplace, wherever you want to be, but you——"

"It's not that," I stammered. "I just——"

"You belong here, girl. Why, Robin, you've made this your home. You love the high country. We can forget. We have to forget. We have to go on." He spoke even more slowly, softly. "I'm not going to let you go."

I felt the tears burn my eyes. My throat choked. I rushed out, hearing Sebastian call, "You cry it out, girl, and decide to listen to the old man."

I made a dash for the stairs, sobbing, trying to choke back my tears. But Michael was just behind me.

"Robin, don't," he said.

I pulled off the wedding ring I had made Jamie buy for me, the false wedding ring. I pulled it off and flung it away. It rolled, twinkling silently on the rug and then disappeared into the shadows.

"Don't you understand?" I cried. "Haven't you figured

it out? Jamie and I weren't married! It was a trick. Nothing more than a con game. And I was part of it. I was going to get my share."

A faint grin touched Michael's face. "I was pretty sure you weren't Jamie's type," he said. "More Sebastian's, I'd say. Or even—even mine, Robin." He paused, went on gently, "The truth is, I'd thought of that as a possibility—one more of Jamie's schemes to get his own way. And I knew if I were right, I could get you safely out of here just by telling Sebastian."

"Why didn't you do it then?"

"Because I saw how he took to you, and I didn't want to spoil it for him, I guess." Michael paused again. "And I suppose, at bottom, not facing it myself, I didn't really want you to leave, Robin." His faint grin died. "I told you—I took too many chances with your life, didn't I?"

"But I can't go on like this, Michael. I can't live with myself any more. Sebastian has to know the truth now."

"He loves you, Robin," Michael said, and added slowly, "and so do I. Surely, you know that." His arms closed around me, drawing me to him. I leaned against him, feeling as if I had come home at last, as if all the sweetest hopeless dreams I'd known were suddenly true.

"Will you forget what's happened, Robin? Forget it all—and forgive me—and stay with us?"

I looked into the hopeful warmth of his gray eyes and knew that he could read my answer in my face. His arms tightened.

"Come on," he said gently. "We'll tell Sebastian there's going to be a real Cromwell bride."

R. F. DELDERFIELD

Sweeping Sagas of Romance and Adventure